# THE
# WITCHES
# OF WORM

## Also by
## ZILPHA KEATLEY SNYDER

# THE
# WITCHES
# OF WORM

Zilpha Keatley Snyder

Illustrated by ALTON RAIBLE

ATHENEUM BOOKS *for* YOUNG READERS

NEW YORK LONDON TORONTO SYDNEY

ATHENEUM BOOKS FOR YOUNG READERS

An imprint of Simon & Schuster Children's Publishing Division

1230 Avenue of the Americas, New York, NY 10020

ATHENEUM BOOKS FOR YOUNG READERS is a registered trademark of Simon & Schuster, Inc.

For information about special discounts for bulk purchases, please contact Simon & Schuster Special Sales at 1-866-506-1949 or business@simonandschuster.com.

The Simon & Schuster Speakers Bureau can bring authors to your live event. For more information or to book an event, contact the Simon & Schuster Speakers Bureau at 1-866-248-3049 or visit our website at www.simonspeakers.com.

Manufactured in the United States of America

This Atheneum hardcover edition September 2009

10 9 8 7 6 5 4 3 2 1

Library of Congress Control Number: 2009903671

ISBN 978-1-4169-9531-9

To Libby,
who is still
gentle and secret,
and to Ruthie,
who left memories
of early magic

# Introduction by the Author

In the early 1970s, just before I began writing *The Witches of Worm*, I started to notice how many young people were using a huge national upsurge of interest in all things "supernatural" in rather negative ways: to attack society in general and their own parents in particular, and to excuse their antisocial behavior by blaming something or somebody else, often their own unhappy childhood or the corrupt society in which they lived. "Something made me do it" had become almost a national alibi.

My initial inspiration for the story came from reading *The Devil in Massachusetts: A Modern Enquiry into the Salem Witch Trials* by Marion L. Starkey. This book contains a carefully documented account of the Salem trials and of the part played in them by Ann Putnam. Ann, who was twelve years old when the accusations began, was the ringleader of the "possessed" children who were ultimately responsible for the deaths of twenty innocent people. In reading the book it occurred to me that many young people of the seventies were, like Ann Putnam, using the beliefs and superstitions of their time to control and manipulate those around them. Like Ann, Jessica in *The Witches of Worm* allows herself to do cruel, even evil things and excuses herself by saying, and almost believing, that "something made me do it"—the "something" in Ann's case being the accused witches, and in Jessica's her "evil" cat.

And in the end? Many years later Ann confessed that she had known she was not possessed, except by her need for attention and power. And at the end of *The Witches of Worm,* Jessica discovers some truths about herself, and about the strange pet whose name is Worm.

*The Witches of Worm* is a serious and in some ways a rather frightening story. I was, at times, frightened by the writing of it. But I believe it includes a message that is no less important today than it was in 1972. The message, as stated by Mrs. Fortune, is that we invite our own devils and we ourselves must exorcise them.

Zilpha Keatley Snyder

# Chapter One

"I'm sorry, Jessie Baby," Joy said.

Jessica looked up from her magazine and stared at her mother, a point-blank unwavering stare that said something important by not saying anything at all. But it didn't matter, because Joy wasn't looking at her anyway.

Joy was looking down into her glass. She was standing over the register in her stocking feet, warming up after a cold ride home from the office in a cable car. Her long blond hair swung down from her bent head, partly covering her face, and the heat from the register made her short skirt stand out like a dancer's tutu. Standing there like that, with one foot tucked up, she looked like a dancer, or else a fashion model—or even a movie star. In fact, according to some people, she

3

looked exactly like one particular star—a sexy blond Swedish actress who played in pictures with English subtitles. Jessica couldn't say about that because the movies were the kind she was too young to get into, but she *was* certain of some other things. She was certain that no one would guess by looking at her, just what Joy really was. No one would suspect that she was only an overworked, underpaid secretary, for instance, and they'd be even less apt to guess that she was Jessica's mother. No one ever believed that at first, because Joy didn't look like anybody's mother, least of all Jessica's. But she was—believe it or not.

My "believe-it-or-not" mother, Jessica thought as she stared at Joy. Sometimes she called her that out loud, but when she did, Joy always seemed to take it as a compliment. Joy had started it herself, actually, by introducing Jessica that way. "And this is my daughter, believe it or not," she would say to people —all kinds of perfect strangers. And none of them ever asked why they might not believe it. Nobody had to ask. It was perfectly obvious why it was hard to believe that Joy could have a twelve-year-old daughter. It was also obvious that, while Joy looked like a Swedish movie star, Jessica did not, and probably never would. But when Jessica called Joy her "believe-it-or-not" mother, she meant something a little different.

Still staring down into her after-work scotch and soda, Joy shook her head slowly and sighed. "I'm really sorry that——" she was beginning again, but Jessica didn't wait to hear the rest of it. She picked up her coat and book and went out the door. She didn't hurry because she knew that Joy was not going to call her back to hear the rest of what she had started to say. Joy would not call her back because they both knew that Jessica knew the rest of it by heart.

If Jessica had waited, Joy would have said one, or all, of a number of things. She would certainly have said she was sorry that, since Alan had asked her out to dinner, there would be a lonely TV dinner for Jessica again that night. Then she might have mentioned some other things she was usually sorry about: that her job kept her away from home until so late, and that they had to live in a city apartment rather than a real house. If she were feeling particularly dramatic, she might have gone on to say that she was sorry she was such a lousy mother, but she guessed she'd never really been cut out for motherhood. Sometimes she even cried a little; Jessica knew that part by heart, too.

Jessica knew it all by heart, and she also knew that none of it was going to change, no matter how sorry Joy might be. Some of the things Joy was sorry about were things she couldn't change even if she wanted to; and most of the rest were things that might have been changed once but that couldn't be now. Like the fact that Jessica Ann Porter had been born twelve years before. That was one of the things it was a lot too late to change.

Halfway down the hallway on the second floor, Jessica stopped, simply from force of habit, to listen to Brandon. If Brandon was at home, he could usually be heard, even when he wasn't practicing his trumpet, as he was obviously doing at the moment. Jessica stood still, listening.

Brandon hadn't been playing the trumpet for very long—only a little over a year. Jessica knew exactly how long it had been because he had started only a short time before the day he had turned into a stinking traitor. She could never forget when that had happened. In that one year Brandon had learned to make the trumpet blare and crow loud enough to disturb everybody for blocks around. Jessica put her hands over her ears, for the shout of the trumpet pierced the walls as if they were tissue paper. It sounded just like Brandon, she thought. He'd always done a lot of shouting.

When she reached the main floor, Jessica walked quickly and quietly. As she passed the Posts' apartment, she could hear a dull whine of conversation and she hurried faster, imagining the door opening and the sound swelling out like a tidal wave to engulf her.

At the rear of the building, passing the door to the apartment where Mrs. Fortune lived with all her cats, she stopped briefly and sniffed to see how bad the cat stink was that evening. Then she went on more quietly, because Mrs. Fortune, in spite of her age, had incredibly good ears. At least, she seemed to know everything that went on in the entire apartment house. But maybe, as Brandon had once suggested, it was only the cats who had good ears, and Mrs. Fortune got her information from them. Jessica could never tell whether Brandon was serious or not when he said weird things like that, but she could believe almost anything about Mrs. Fortune. She was that kind of person.

Outside the rear entrance to the apartment house, Jessica stopped and stood still, breathing deeply. Sometimes it made things seem better if she could get away and breathe long slow breaths of outside air. But today it only made things worse.

It was a terrible day, dank and windy—the kind of chilling August day that often betrayed the city's tourists, sending them shivering home to their hotels in their light summer coats. Jessica coughed and shoved her whipping hair back out of her face. The air tasted gray and poisonous, heavy with fog and city smells, and the sound of the wind was sad and angry as it swept down the alley and around the walls and fences of the Regency Apartment House. There was something threatening about the sound, as if the whining moan was full of strange half-spoken words. Shivering, Jessica buttoned the top button of her coat, shoved her book into a pocket, and hurried across the yard.

The back yard of the Regency was small and, except for a narrow strip near the building, very steep. The steepness was a part of the sharp rise that soared up directly behind the apartment house, up to a flat hilltop known as Blackberry Heights. Some of the most expensive houses in the city were in Blackberry Heights, and Joy was always wishing that she and Jessica could afford to live there. But since there was no hope of that, the next best thing was to live at the foot of the Heights, where you could share in some of the advantages. There were, for instance, the advantages of good schools and a good address. That was what Joy said. As far as Jessica was concerned, the main advantage was having a cliff for a back yard.

Beyond the cat-proof fence that enclosed the Regency's private patch of hillside, the slope of the cliff became very steep and wild. Only weeds and ugly scratchy bushes grew there, struggling for a roothold in the almost vertical stone. A climber struggled, too, slipping and sliding, unless he knew the secret footholds, dug in the distant past by Jessica and Brandon. Anyone who knew those holds and followed them carefully halfway up the face of the cliff, came upon the entrance to the secret cave. That was where Jessica was going.

As she reached the last foothold and boosted herself up to the threshold of the cave, Jessica turned suddenly and peered downward, shading her eyes with her palm. Her face tightened into an expression of terror,

and her voice shook as she said, "They're still following. They've found the entrance to the pass."

Moving quickly backward, she assumed a different expression, concerned but calm now, and determined.

"Courage lad!" Her voice had deepened. "We still have one ace in the hole. Roll out the catapult."

Switching back into the part of a frightened boy, she began, "Oh, sir, there's hundreds of them. And they have spears and crossbows and——" She stopped then, in mid-sentence, with a shrug and a disgusted laugh.

"Idiot," she said in her own voice. She had to be an idiot to go on playing those silly games. It had been dumb enough that she had done it when she was younger and was just going along with Brandon's crazy ideas. But to keep on doing it—as she did now and then—all by herself! She shook her head. "You're really cracking up, Jessie Baby," she told herself.

Sitting down on a ledge, she looked around. The cave had not changed at all since her last visit. A natural crevice, hardly more than five feet deep, it was just high enough to stand up in. Jessica and Brandon had used it in a lot of their games. It had been Injun Joe's cave, the Open Sesame cave, and many others. Once they had planned to enlarge it and turn it into a real cavern, but days of digging had produced only a tiny closetlike addition, so the project had been abandoned. They had gone on using the cave, though, until Brandon had given it up, along with everything else they had shared together.

The cave was just Jessica's now, and she still went there from time to time—not really to play stupid games anymore, but usually just to have a quiet place to read. Reading was one useful thing left over from her friendship with Brandon. That was what their games had been really—acted-out stories from books. Jessica had read so many of them to learn her parts that she had developed the habit—the habit of reading just about everything. And it was a good thing, too, considering how little else she had to do anymore.

The reading spot was a natural stone shelf padded with old blankets. It was near the mouth of the cave, where one could look out through the straggly bushes and see the Regency Apartment House almost directly below. By leaning forward she could see the rear windows of all the apartments in the main building and the shingled roof of the small one-story wing where Mrs. Fortune lived. Jessica sat there often, looking down at the windows, imagining what everyone inside was doing, and wondering what kinds of things might happen to them all someday.

Sometimes she made up long stories about the future. There was one where she came back to the Regency, after having become rich and famous. She had just purchased the whole block, and as the new owner of the Regency, she had come to tell the Posts that they were fired. She told Mrs. Fortune she could stay if she got rid of the cats, and she told the Doyles that they were being evicted because of Brandon; he was guilty of noise pollution. There was another part about going up to the third floor to see Joy. Joy looked different, older and not so blond. Jessica told her about the beautiful big house in Blackberry Heights that she had just moved into. She suggested that Joy come and visit sometimes. Of course, it would have to be when she, Jessica, wasn't away making a TV show or something like that. Joy was very eager to come, and she said things about how lonely she had been since Jessica went away and got famous.

Jessica knew it was really a childish thing to do—making up stupid daydreams like that, and she sometimes made fun of herself about it. "Come on, Jessie Baby," she'd say to herself—she always called herself Jessie Baby when she was disgusted—"Come on, Jessie Baby. Let's quit wasting time with fairy tales like that Rich-and-Famous stuff." But sometimes she did it, anyway.

Today she started in the middle with the part about evicting Brandon. But even though it was one of the best parts—she'd been adding to it and improving it for over a year—she found that she was unable to keep her mind on it. Things kept happening to distract her.

Some of the distraction was only a feeling, a restless uneasy feeling that made her waste long moments watching and listening, without the slightest idea of what she was watching for. But some of the distraction was caused by the weather.

Jessica had never been in the secret cave on such a strange day. As she watched, far off toward the bay a huge dark cloud bank began to grow and spread. Closer in, the wind caught a spreading ooze of fog and wrapped it clean around the Regency Apartment House like an enormous cloak, and then raveled it into snaky fingers that writhed off around corners and down alleys. The wind moaned and cried and then quieted into a furtive stealthy whisper until Jessica found herself straining to hear its secret. Finally she gave up on the daydream and decided to see if it would be any easier to keep her mind on reading.

She was settling herself more comfortably on her stomach on the shelf when she realized she could still hear the faint throbbing wail of Brandon's trumpet. Scooting forward she picked out the window of the Doyles' apartment. Either Brandon was standing near an open window or he was learning to play louder than ever. The sound of the trumpet had never reached her in the secret cave before, but now it came again and again, pulsing up through the city noises like a faint and far away shout. Still shouting, Jessica thought.

Brandon had shouted at Jessica the first time they met. That was when they were both only five years old. It had happened in the back yard of the Regency, not long after the Doyles had moved in. Jessica had lived there for as long as she could remember, but until Brandon came she had been the only child. Then one morning when she was five, she had come out the back door and found a boy building something on the sidewalk out of a lot of old spools and blocks. She had never seen the boy before, but she had recognized the building materials at once. They were from a box of interesting things that Mrs. Fortune called her Treasure Chest. The chest was kept in a hall closet and was brought out for Jessica to play with when she came to visit. Mrs. Fortune said that many, many children had played with the things in the box. But for a long time there had been no one but Jessica.

It was probably because it had always been her Treasure Chest, and also because Brandon ignored her, that she had gotten mad. He was so busy stacking her spools into a tall tower that he didn't notice her, even when she had made some warning noises. So she had run right through the middle of his building, knocking it to pieces. He had noticed her then. Shouting at the top of his voice, he had run after her and hit her on the head with his fist.

She hadn't cried. Jessica never cried—not even then at the age of five. She had not cried or hit back or even shouted. Instead she had quietly said some things to Brandon—some of the worst words she knew. Before she had finished, Brandon had stopped shouting and begun to listen. When she had run out of things to call him and begun to back away, suddenly he wasn't mad anymore. He had rubbed his nose with his knuckles and the strange high intensity had come into his eyes. A look, she found out later, that meant he was curious or interested.

"Say that again," he had said.

"Say what again?" Jessica had asked.

"All of it," Brandon had said. "All of what you just said."

"Why? It means something very bad."

"Yeah?" Brandon had looked even more intrigued. "What? What does it mean?"

Jessica had shrugged. "Something very bad. My mother says it when she's very mad."

"Why don't you ask her?"

"I did. She won't tell me."

Brandon had nodded. "Hey," he had then said, "do you want to help me build a castle?" Just as if he hadn't been yelling and hitting a minute before.

That was the way he was then and the way he always was. You could never predict anything about Brandon—what would make him angry, what would make him laugh, or what crazy thing he'd decide to do next. But if you were never sure about what would happen next, at least you were always sure about what was happening at the moment. You never had to wonder, for instance, if he was angry or not. When Brandon was angry, you found out immediately. But then he didn't stay angry. And afterward everything was the same as it had been before. He was weird that way—different.

Even his looks were weird. He was thick and

slow-moving, with a face that seemed to slant in too many directions. But his hands and eyes were different, as if they belonged to somebody else. His eyes were dark blue with bushy gold-colored lashes, and they were always changing flickering shades of blue, as if a blue fire burned inside. And his hands were long and narrow and good at everything from digging holes to drawing pictures.

His likes were weird, too. He liked a lot of crazy things: book games, or "plays" as he called them, instead of real games like baseball or checkers. He liked music, even old-fashioned symphony stuff, and strange people: Mrs. Fortune for example. And sometimes he disliked things for crazy reasons. You could count on Brandon to be crazy and unpredictable and exciting. Jessica had counted on it, for more than five years.

The faint liquid sound of the trumpet died away at last, and she turned back to her book. It was a new one that she had just checked out of the library. It was called *The Witches of Salem Town*, and it was not really a story at all. Instead it was a true account of events that happened a long time ago. As a rule Jessica preferred fiction, but there had recently been an article about witches in one of the women's magazines that Joy subscribed to, and Jessica had been fascinated. Afterward she had gone looking for more information at the library. In the children's section she had found only cutesy stories about Halloween-type witches with cats and broomsticks; but when she discovered where the adult books on magic were kept, she found what she was looking for. The book she had taken was a brand-new one that told the story of the witches of Salem.

The first few chapters of the book turned out to be mostly about a girl who had lived in Salem and who, at the time of the witches, was just twelve years old. Her name was Ann, which was Jessica's own middle name. Ann had become the most famous of the people who accused the witches. She had been so important that many famous people came to talk to her, and everyone pitied or feared or admired her. Afterward many books and papers were written about her and the Salem witch trials.

As Jessica read, she kept turning back to look at a picture in the front of the book. It was a picture of a dim, old-fashioned drawing that showed a girl lying on the floor and reaching up with one hand. Many people were gathered around, looking down at her. The girl's face was only partly visible, but it seemed to be thin and rather dark.

By the time Jessica finished reading the first three chapters, the light in the cave had become very dim, and the print seemed to squirm before her eyes. She was reading about the demons who had tormented Ann and the other girls, and she wanted desperately to find out what happened next, but at last her eyes ached so badly from straining to make out the words in the failing light that she was forced to stop. She closed her eyes to rest them only for a moment, and although she did not remember feeling at all sleepy, she was almost instantly asleep and dreaming.

It was almost dark in the cave when Jessica awoke. She lay still, feeling the dream seeping away into the dark parts of her mind. Keeping her eyes closed, she tried desperately to push her thoughts backward to grasp the fluttering fragments of the dreams and hold them. But they continued to fade, tantalizingly close to the edge of consciousness, until nothing was left but a vague shadowy scene and the memory of a fierce and frightening excitement. There had been a room in the dream, an enormous room glowing darkly with shining wood. And there had been people, many strangers with blurred faces, and some who were vaguely familiar, except that they seemed to be wearing masks carved from ice, which had frozen their faces into exaggerated expressions of fear. The rest of the dream was gone, except for an echo of violent noises and the feeling of fierce excitement.

When she finally gave up trying to remember more, Jessica sat up and peered out and down at the apartment house. Windows were lighted now in all the apartments, including her own on the third floor. Joy would be gone on her date with Alan, but the lights had been left on, and undoubtedly Mrs. Post had been notified that Jessica would be home alone. Sometime during the evening Mrs. Post would be up to find out how Jessica was doing, and to gather any other information she could possibly uncover.

What would happen, Jessica wondered, if she should decide to spend the whole night in the secret cave? Mrs. Post would arrive, pushing her heavy way up the two flights of stairs, to find no sign of Jessica. What would she do? What would Joy do when she came home to find her "believe-it-or-not" daughter had completely disappeared? Perhaps it was a good night to find out.

It would be a cold night though, cold and damp. The wind had died down, but the fog had settled in, deeper and more chill. The air smelled, now, of wet stones and moldy earth, as if it had come oozing up from caves and graveyards instead of blowing in from the open sea. Above, the sky was a sooty gray, but near the earth a layer of dusky light lingered, as if the day were trying desperately to stay alive.

In the thick muffling fog there was a strange difference in the quality of sound. All the usual sounds that could be heard from the secret cave, city sounds of horns and traffic, seemed distant and indistinct, fragmented by hollow echoes.

Jessica was leaning forward, listening intently, when a lull came in the flow of city sounds, a trough of silence between waves of noise, and into the silence another sound intruded. It was a soft and secret sound of movement, a crawling scrabbling noise, and it was very, very near. Jessica jumped to her feet and whirled to face the back of the cave.

# Chapter Two

THE BACK OF THE CAVE WAS IN DEEP SHADOW, AND for the first few seconds Jessica could see nothing at all. Then, as she inched forward, she saw a deeper shadow that moved slowly and fitfully on the stony floor. At first she thought it was a snake, but as she edged closer, she could make out tiny feet reaching out to scratch helplessly at the hard stone.

At last, her fright dwindling, Jessica squatted directly above the squirming object, but even then she was not entirely sure that it was only a kitten. For one thing, it was much smaller than any kitten she had ever seen before, and for another, it did not meow or make any sort of cry. Even when she finally brought herself to poke it gingerly in the side with one finger, it made no sound at all.

"It's almost dead, I guess," she told herself, but as she went on watching, it continued to move, trying to pull itself forward over the hard bare ground. It occurred to Jessica that its mother must have brought it to the cave and abandoned it, since no one else knew about the secret cave and very few people could climb to it even if they knew. Jessica had heard of a mother cat refusing to accept a kitten. Perhaps, in such cases, the mother carried it away and left it in a hidden place to die. She reached out and touched the kitten tentatively on its tiny back.

She had never liked cats. There were a number of reasons why. One was, of course, that she had had to live so long at the Regency, where Mrs. Fortune's cats smelled up the back yard and half the building. All the tenants talked about the cat smell, but no one could do anything about it because the apartment house really belonged to Mrs. Fortune. Mr. Post took care of things and served as landlord, but that was only because Mrs. Fortune was too old and too busy with her cats.

But Mrs. Fortune's cats were not the only reason Jessica had never liked cats. Actually she had always much preferred dogs, but Joy wouldn't let her have one. Joy was afraid of dogs, although she wouldn't admit it, and insisted that cats were better for apartment living. Joy often said that Jessica should have a kitten to keep her company when she was home alone. But Jessica had made it clear, time after time, that a cat was not what she wanted.

Now, however, like it or not, Jessica knew something had to be done about the tiny abandoned kitten. Even if for no other reason than to keep it from dying there and smelling up the cave. Eventually she reached out gingerly and picked it up.

It felt strange in her hands, unlike any kitten she had touched before. Its tiny body was firm and supple with very little of the fluffy softness a kitten is supposed to have. It writhed in her hands with surprising strength, and turned its incredibly small face up to hers. As she moved with it to the mouth of the cave, she saw with horror that it had no eyes. For an instant she came very close to throwing it down the cliff, but instead she quickly shoved it into the pocket of her coat, put her book in the other pocket, and began the downward climb. When she reached the apartment house, she went directly to the door of Mrs. Fortune's apartment.

To be knocking on that door again seemed strange. For a long time, she'd knocked there almost every day, by herself at first and then with Brandon. In those days, a visit to Mrs. Fortune's had been a favorite thing to do. But she hadn't been there much lately.

Joy had never liked it. "Spending so much time with that weird old woman," she said. "I don't understand it. What does she have in that smelly apartment of hers—a gingerbread house?"

There had never been a gingerbread house, but

there had been reasons. One was simply that Mrs. Fortune was often the only person home in the whole apartment building, except for Mrs. Post—and no one who didn't have to, would ever visit Mrs. Post. But there were other reasons, too. There was the Treasure Chest, full of dozens of interesting old things, some of them so old that Mrs. Fortune had played with them herself as a child. There was an old crank-up phonograph and a stock of scratchy-voiced records; and there were hundreds of strange old books, stacked and crammed onto dusty shelves. And then, too, there was Mrs. Fortune herself.

Mrs. Fortune had always been pleased to have visitors, even when she was having one of the strange spells that made people say she was losing her mind. At those times she would not answer questions, but would sit with her head nodding gently, talking to herself or to one of her white cats. At other times she was quite different, lively and talkative and very interested in everything that Brandon and Jessica said and did. Once in a while she would even tell them stories.

Mrs. Fortune's stories were as strange as she was. They were always about impossible things like talking animals or magical objects, and she told them as if they really happened—and to her. When Jessica was very young, she had really believed in Mrs. Fortune's stories, and Brandon had, too. In fact, Brandon had never stopped believing them, or at least pretending to. Right up until a year ago, when Jessica had stopped speaking to him, Brandon had still talked as if he believed that Mrs. Fortune could do all sorts of supernatural things. He probably still believed it. At least he still visited Mrs. Fortune now and then.

The door opened, and Mrs. Fortune, smiling her old face into a network of wrinkles, said, "Well, Jessica. What a surprise. Won't you come in?"

She looked terribly old, older than forever, and her faded dress of heavy brown material hung loosely on her thin body. Her long gray hair was tied at the back of her neck with a piece of string. People had always talked about Mrs. Fortune's strange appearance, but Jessica had never paid much attention to it. Now, suddenly, she found herself thinking, She does look weird. It's a good thing for her she doesn't live in Salem in the olden days. But out loud she only said, "Hello, Mrs. Fortune. I've come about this."

She pulled the kitten out of her pocket and held it out. "I thought maybe you might want it."

Mrs. Fortune leaned forward, peering. "Good gracious, child. It's a newborn kitten. Where on earth did you get it?"

"Out by the hill," Jessica said. "It was abandoned. I thought maybe you could raise it."

Mrs. Fortune reached out and took the kitten. Her thin, crooked old fingers closed around it like the claws of a huge bird. "But it's much too young to be taken from its mother," she said. "It's very difficult to raise a kitten this young by hand. If I had a nursing mother, I could try to get her to accept it, but none of my cats have kittens now."

She moved back out of the dimly lighted doorway to hold the kitten under the glow of the table lamp.

"My word," she said. "It's an ugly little thing, isn't it? And such a strange color."

In the strong light the kitten had become a chalky gray, the color of dead ashes. Its fur was so short and fine that its wiry body seemed to be almost hairless.

"It's blind, too." Jessica could hardly bear to look at the kitten's blank unfinished face.

"Yes, but of course that's only temporary," Mrs. Fortune said. "Its eyes will open when it is about ten days old."

"Oh, yeah," Jessica said. Actually she'd forgotten, if she'd ever known, that kittens were born blind. She had been thinking of the kitten's eyelessness as some horrible abnormality.

"Come, my dear," Mrs. Fortune said. "Let's see if we can get it to eat." In her crowded little kitchen that smelled strongly of cat food, Mrs. Fortune got out a small can of milk and a tiny doll's bottle. She heated the milk and added a drop of liquid vitamins. Then she poured the warm milk into the bottle.

But the kitten refused to eat. It didn't cry or struggle, just turned its blind face determinedly away from the bottle, time after time. At last the phone rang, and Mrs. Fortune put the kitten in Jessica's lap and went to answer it. Jessica sat and watched it squirming there for a while, but finally she picked up the bottle and held it to the kitten's mouth. Immediately it opened its mouth, took the nipple, and began to suck. By the time Mrs. Fortune had returned, the bottle was half empty.

"Ahh," she said. "Good for you. I'm glad you decided to try. This may well be your last chance."

It was the kind of weird thing Mrs. Fortune sometimes said. In the midst of an ordinary conversation, she would suddenly make a remark that sounded as if it were meant for an entirely different person. Mrs. Post was always telling people about the strange things Mrs. Fortune said, and how she, herself, always pretended she hadn't heard so as not to embarrass the poor old soul. But Jessica had always been too curious to pretend.

"What do you mean—'your last chance'?" she asked. "Are you talking to the kitten, or to me?"

Mrs. Fortune chuckled appreciatively, as if Jessica had said something very witty. "Perhaps the kitten," she said. "Perhaps it hasn't very many lives left."

"Oh, you mean like a cat having nine lives? Do you really think they do?"

"Ahh," Mrs. Fortune said, chuckling again, "sometimes I'm sure of it. Now this kitten, for instance, has surely lived before. He's much too wise, I think, for only a few days of life. Don't you agree?" She picked up the kitten and began to rub under its tail with a wet cloth.

"He doesn't look very wise to me," Jessica said.

"What are you doing to him?"

"I'm helping him to eliminate. The mother cat does this by washing. Many people who try to raise very young kittens allow them to die because they don't know this is necessary. It must be done until their eyes are open and they begin to walk."

"Ugh," Jessica said when Mrs. Fortune had finished. "I'm glad that's over."

Mrs. Fortune smiled. "But it is only over for the moment. It will all have to be done again in two hours, and every two hours for two weeks. After that the time between feedings can be lengthened."

"Every two hours," Jessica said. "That's impossible."

"Not impossible, but very difficult. I have raised kittens that way several times in the past, but I was younger and stronger then. I wouldn't be able to do it now. If I were awakened every two hours now, I wouldn't be able to sleep at all."

"What am I supposed to do then," Jessica said. "I don't want a kitten. I don't even like cats."

Mrs. Fortune nodded her shaky old head. "Then perhaps you can find someone who has a nursing mother cat who might accept this poor orphan. Surely among your school friends someone would know of a cat with kittens."

"Well, I don't know."

"Why don't you try? I'll give you the bottle and some milk, and you can take the kitten up to your apartment while you call your friends. Then perhaps tomorrow you can take him to his new home."

There wasn't anything more for Jessica to say. Mrs. Fortune obviously didn't want the kitten, and Jessica wasn't going to explain that there wasn't anyone she could call to ask about mother cats. Reluctantly she took the padded box that Mrs. Fortune had prepared with the kitten tucked in beside a quart jar of warm water, and returned to her own apartment.

It wasn't until she was through eating her TV dinner, a tasteless veal cutlet, that she discovered that the new book about Salem was no longer in her pocket. It must have fallen out, she decided, while she was climbing down the hill, or else in Mrs. Fortune's apartment. Wherever it was, it would have to stay there until morning, and that meant that she had nothing to read. She shuffled through the stack of magazines on the end table without any luck. She had already finished everything of interest in them. That left only television. But that seldom appealed to her, particularly when she was home alone. She turned on the set and threw herself angrily onto the couch.

Not long afterward, Mrs. Post arrived to "look in" on Jessica. "Looking in" on everybody and everything was Mrs. Post's favorite occupation. When Jessica had gotten too old to need a baby-sitter, Joy had started letting the Posts know when Jessica was going to be home alone, just in case of an emergency. But the "looking in" part was Mrs. Post's own idea.

Jessica yelled "come in" without getting up off the couch; and Mrs. Post lumberėd in and lowered herself onto her favorite chair, the little ladder-backed one by the telephone. Jessica guessed she liked it because she could get off it again a little easier than she could the lower and softer ones. But the little chair did a lot of creaking whenever Mrs. Post sat on it, and Jessica always expected it to collapse in splinters.

"Just thought I'd look in a minute, dear, to be sure you're safe and well."

"I'm fine," Jessica said, turning her eyes reluctantly away from the TV toward Mrs. Post. She wasn't at all interested in the program, but she wasn't interested in one of Mrs. Post's lectures, either.

"What are you watching, dear?"

"A play," Jessica said. "An old play about some weird people."

Mrs. Post glanced at the set for a moment. "Well," she said, "I suppose it's suitable for a twelve-year-old. I suppose your mother must have approved it. Of course, with her away so much these days, it must be hard for her to keep track of what you watch. I do think——"

"Excuse me, Mrs. Post," Jessica said, getting up off the couch. "I have to go to the bathroom." In the bathroom she locked the door and leaned on the basin, making faces at herself in the mirror. First she sucked in her cheeks and narrowed her long eyes. Joy, whose face was round and soft-looking around the edges, said that Jessica had a foxy face. Jessica bared her teeth, making herself look more foxlike, sly and angry—an angry fox face. Then she pulled her eyebrows together and puffed her cheeks way out. "I do think——" she said in a perfect imitation of Mrs. Post's voice—not quite as loud as a power saw but just as whiny and annoying. "I do think that children are left to their own devices too much these days. Now when my children were small——"

Jessica was great at imitations. Even Brandon said so. In fact, Brandon had been the first one to mention it. He used to laugh at her imitations of people they knew, particularly Mrs. Post. But once he'd almost slugged her for imitating Mrs. Fortune's shaky head.

After a few minutes, Jessica flushed the toilet and went back into the living room. Mrs. Post was still there, but at least she was on her feet again. As she went out the door, she reminded Jessica to keep the door locked when she was home alone.

"You really must keep the door locked, Jessica," she said for the hundredth time. "To leave the door unlocked and just call 'come in' the way you do is terribly dangerous. You never know, these days, who might walk in."

"I knew it was you," Jessica said. She stared at Mrs. Post thinking, I knew it was you because no one else makes the stairs creak like that. She didn't say it out loud, but Mrs. Post must have guessed what she was

31

thinking because she frowned and her face got a little red.

When she was gone, Jessica got up and locked the door. Mrs. Post had been expecting a murderer at the Regency Apartment House for as long as Jessica could remember. He hadn't appeared yet, but Jessica wasn't at all sure he wouldn't someday. It was just that she didn't intend to lock the door before Mrs. Post made her inevitable appearance. She wasn't about to get up and go to the door to let Mrs. Post in every single night, when she didn't want her to come in the first place. So she just had to take her chances on the murderer until after Mrs. Post had come and gone.

With Mrs. Post out of the way, Jessica went to the kitchen and looked at the kitten. It had been almost two hours since Mrs. Fortune had fed and cleaned it. It was moving restlessly on the bottom of the box, a squirming hairless blob. There was a shapeless unborn look about it that made her shiver.

"Ugh," she said. "You squirmy thing. Why should I waste my time keeping you alive? I don't want you."

At the sound of her voice, the wobbly weaving head steadied. The kitten lay still, listening and waiting.

"I don't want you," Jessica repeated loudly. Angrily, she jerked a pan out of the cupboard and slammed it onto the stove. When the milk was heated, she filled the bottle, and sitting down on the floor, she picked the kitten up with the tips of her fingers and put it in her lap. It drank fiercely, concentrating all the

strength of its tiny body on food until the last drop of milk was gone.

Shortly afterward, when Jessica got into bed, she did a very unusual thing—she reached over and turned out the light. She never turned out the light or went to sleep when Joy was still out, no matter how late it got to be. Instead she sat up in bed, reading or only thinking, until she heard Joy's key in the lock. Then she turned out the light quickly and flopped down under the covers. When Joy looked in a few minutes later, she would pretend to be fast asleep. By lying in a certain position with her head propped on the pillow, she could see the doorway through squinted eyes.

Joy would stand still a moment, usually, and the light from the hallway would turn her blond hair into a shining wreath, and her face would be shadowed and very beautiful. Once, when Jessica was about eight years old, Joy had come into the room and kissed her very softly on the forehead. But usually she only stood in the doorway and then tiptoed away. After that Jessica would go to sleep.

There was no longer any real reason why Jessica stayed awake until Joy got home, but there had been once. There had been a time when she was afraid to go to sleep because of a dream that came back again and again. It was a terrifying dream about waking up all alone in an empty room that grew bigger and emptier until it filled the whole universe. She had

34

not had the dream for a long time, but waiting up for Joy had become a habit.

There was no reason to break the habit for the first time on that particular night. Of course, she had nothing to read, but that had happened before. The only thing different was the kitten and he was certainly not a very good reason to do anything, except that if she were asleep at the next feeding time, she wouldn't have to decide what to do.

So Jessica turned out the lights and settled down to sleep, and she did *not* set the alarm, as Mrs. Fortune had suggested. Perhaps she would wake up and perhaps she wouldn't. She didn't much care either way. If the kitten was dead in the morning, the problem would be solved.

It was almost exactly two hours later that Jessica found herself suddenly wide awake and staring through the darkness at the luminous hands of her clock. At first she thought she had heard something, maybe Joy arriving home, but she waited and listened without hearing the familiar sounds of clicking high heels and doors opening and closing. But there *had* been something like a sound.

Closing her eyes and using all her energy to listen, Jessica began to hear it again—the same breath-soft sound of movement she had heard in the cave. She couldn't possibly hear that cat moving, yet she was sure she did. She also obviously couldn't see anything,

35

but a kind of picture kept forming behind her tightly closed eyelids.

She saw a face, triangular and ashy gray, but instead of being blind and eyeless, it seemed to be mostly eyes. The top part of the face was filled with two huge glowing diamonds. Jessica blinked hard and the face disappeared, only to return with the diamond eyes glowing brighter than before. At last she turned on the lights and jumped out of bed.

When Jessica bent over the cardboard box in the corner of the kitchen, the kitten raised its head and sniffed the air. It turned its face toward her, wrinkled its flat nose, and sniffed again. It was, of course, as blind as ever. But when its weaving head faced Jessica directly, it stopped. It clearly knew that she was there, and it knew exactly where—but it did not call to her to feed it. It only went on watching her blindly, waiting for what she would do.

# Chapter Three

JESSICA HADN'T MEANT TO FEED THE KITTEN AGAIN. She had gotten out of bed and gone into the kitchen just to look at it for a moment. Not that she wanted to see it. It was almost as if it seemed dangerous not to, in the same strange way that it sometimes seemed very dangerous to step on a crack or walk under a ladder, or follow some other silly superstition.

But once in the kitchen, faced with that strange blind watchfulness, Jessica found herself refilling the hot-water bottle and heating the milk. The kitten was still drinking when Joy finally returned from her date with Alan.

Jessica was sitting on the kitchen floor with the kitten in her lap, supporting its tiny body in an almost vertical position. The bottle was nearly empty when there was the sound of a key in the front door, whispered words, and then Joy appearing in the kitchen doorway.

Joy was wearing her velvet dress with the high waist that made her look like a medieval princess. Her golden hair was pulled up into a curly ponytail, and her cheeks were very red. She was humming a tune until she saw Jessica, and then she jumped and looked startled—almost guilty.

"Jessie," she said. "What on earth? What are you doing awake at this hour?"

Jessica could have said, "I'm always awake at this hour on nights you're away," but she didn't. Instead she only said, "I'm feeding a kitten. It has to eat every two hours."

"A kitten!" Joy looked amazed and then pleased. "I thought you hated cats. Here, let's have a look." She crossed the kitchen unsteadily and bent over Jessica. "Let me see the itsy-bitsy——" She was going on in the crooning baby talk she always used when she spoke to cats, but she stopped in mid-croon. "Good Lord! Jessica, are you sure that's a kitten? It doesn't look like any kitten I've ever seen."

"It's very young," Jessica said. "Maybe only a couple of days. That's why it has to be fed so often. It's not really old enough to leave its mother."

"Well, let's take it back to its mother then, and we'll get you one of those darling Persians from the pet shop."

"I don't want a darling Persian," Jessica said.

"That's ridiculous," Joy said. "If you want a kitten, let's get you a good one, instead of that poor little monster. It hardly looks like a kitten at all."

"It's a kitten," Jessica said.

"Well, I suppose it must be, but look how bare and squirmy it is." Joy drew up her shoulders in a delicate shudder. "It reminds me of some kind of worm. A poor little blind worm."

"I like worms," Jessica said. "I like worms a lot better than kittens."

So its name was Worm, and Jessica continued to take care of it, although she didn't know why. Fortunately, for Worm at least, summer vacation wasn't over or she wouldn't have been able to do it even if she'd wanted to. And she didn't want to, not really, but something—a strange unwilling kind of fascination—kept her coming back to peer into the box in the kitchen. And once there, the kitten's inescapable blind watchfulness held her like a charm until it was fed and cared for.

Sometimes, dragging herself out of bed in the middle of the night, Jessica would decide that the very next day she would take the kitten to the animal shelter and leave it. Of course they would put it to sleep. No one would want to raise such a useless ugly kitten. But somehow Jessica never got around to going to the animal shelter.

It was during those night feedings that Jessica began to talk to Worm. Staggering out of her warm bed, blinking in the sudden glare of the kitchen lights, she would grab him out of his box and hold him in both hands.

"Yes," she would say. "Here I am, you awful pest. I suppose you think I like having to get up at all hours to take care of a disgusting thing like you. I suppose you think I enjoy having to hold you while you drool milk all over me and having to clean your bottom like a dirty baby. If I start getting sick or something, it's going to be your fault. It's not good for somebody my age to miss so much sleep. Just like it's your fault I lost that brand-new library book and now I'm going to have to pay for it out of my own allowance, and I never even got to finish reading it. I should have just let you die, even if it is your ninth life, like Mrs. Fortune said."

Other times, Jessica would come into the kitchen and sit down beside the box and talk to Worm without touching him at all. "Why don't you cry?" she'd ask him. "It's past your eating time. Why don't you meow like an ordinary kitten and ask me for your food?"

Always, when Jessica talked to him, Worm would push himself up waveringly to a sitting position and turn his face toward hers. He would sit waiting, listening, moving with her every move, until she was sure that, in some weird way, he could see her from behind his blind eyes.

"Why don't you cry?" Jessica would ask, and then she would answer for him.

"Why should I cry like an ordinary cat?" she'd imagine him saying. "I am Worm, and I am different."

"Ugh," Jessica would answer. "You're different, all right—uglier and weirder."

"I am different," Worm would say. "Mrs. Fortune knows. She told you I was wise."

"All I know is that you're a disgusting little monster. Come here and drink your milk so I can get back to bed."

It took a long time for Worm to get his eyes. Mrs. Fortune had said that kittens' eyes open slowly, a little bit at a time; but more than a week passed, and there was still not the slightest crack in the tight gray creases that slanted upward from each side of the flat nose. Jessica was beginning to think she'd been right in the first place—that there was something abnormal about that strange unfinished face.

But then, one morning, she slept through a feeding and hurried into the kitchen just after daybreak to find Worm sitting up in the corner of his box, watching her through slits that widened into blue-black diamonds.

"Well," she said, snatching him up and giving him a shake. "So you did have real eyes all the time."

Worm opened his tiny red cavern of a mouth and

hissed at her like an angry snake. Jessica had not seen him do that before, and for a moment she felt almost frightened, but then she shrugged. "I don't like your looks either," she said. "So I guess we're even."

By the time school started, Worm had graduated to being fed only every four hours. By coming home at lunch time, Jessica was able to maintain his feeding schedule. The school was only four blocks away, and though she had never bothered to come home for lunch before, this year, eating lunch at home actually worked out rather well. It worked out well because there was no one at school with whom Jessica could eat. Not right at the moment, anyway, since she'd lost two of her best friends during the summer. Or, to be more exact, she had lost the only two friends she had—the only ones since Brandon.

Brandon had never been a school friend because he had always gone to a private school. Not having anyone at school then hadn't mattered much as long as there were afternoons and weekends with Brandon to think about and plan for. But when Brandon wasn't a friend anymore, Jessica had decided to work at finding somebody at school. It had taken a long time and a lot of effort to discover Diane and Alise; and now since the middle of summer, they were gone, too.

Alise, who had been stubborn and bossy anyway, and who had only been friendly between fights, had moved away in the middle of June. Then, early in August, Diane, who was not too exciting but very easy to get along with, had deserted Jessica for a new red-haired girl named Brenda, who lived on the Heights and who had a private swimming pool. So Jessica had been left with no one and nothing—except a whole lot of free time.

There was another reason for the recent increase in Jessica's spare time—Alan, Joy's newest boyfriend. Joy had had quite a few boyfriends, but most of them had come and gone. Alan, however, seemed to be different. He had been around for several months, and Joy had been seeing more and more of him. Joy had told Jessica that she felt Alan was serious, which meant that he might be considering marriage.

Jessica supposed she couldn't blame Joy for being interested in a man who was thinking of marriage. As she was always pointing out, she had never really had a husband to help her with all the difficulties of mak- a living and raising a child. She had gotten married when she was "ridiculously young," and when she was still only eighteen and the mother of a newborn baby, Jessica's father had run away and deserted them both. Jessica had heard all about Joy's problems so many times that she couldn't help seeing how great it was that Alan was the marrying type—except that nothing had ever happened to make Jessica think he was the least bit the father type. Alan looked very young, and it was easy to guess that if he ever did get interested in being a father, it wouldn't be of someone who was already twelve years old.

So that was the way things had been lately. First, cross out Brandon, and then Alise and Diane, and finally Joy, too, which left only—Worm. Jessica had to admit that if Worm had to happen to her, he couldn't have picked a better time. In any other year, she would never have had the time to spend on keeping him alive. But she did have time now, a great deal of it, and as the days went by, she went on spending it on Worm.

# Chapter Four

As THE WEEKS PASSED, WORM GREW RAPIDLY. JESSICA watched him, waiting for him to arrive at the round and cuddly stage—the toy-faced cute stage that all kittens go through. But although his eyes widened and grew into enormous slanted diamonds and he learned to slither or spring on his lengthening legs, his cuddly kitten stage did not arrive. He grew larger and larger, but he remained slick and silent, worm-thin and worm-gray.

Joy, who had always claimed to love cats, didn't seem to like Worm any better as he started looking more like a cat and less like a "blind gray worm." She went on mentioning to Jessica all the things that were wrong with him and how much better it would have been to get a Persian from the pet shop.

"I'm sure that losing his mother at such an early

45

age must have damaged him in some way," Joy said. "He doesn't seem like a normal kitten at all. He's so ugly and unfriendly, and he doesn't romp around the way a normal kitten does."

"He plays," Jessica said. "He just doesn't do it when you're around. No wonder he hides when you're here. He probably thinks you're a stranger—you're gone so much."

Jessica didn't mention that Worm seldom played when she herself was around, either. She knew he played only because she heard him. At least she thought that was what he was doing—running madly around the apartment at night after she was in bed. A few times she had caught him springing or running when she entered a room, but as soon as he saw her, he stopped and sat still, watching and waiting, as always. Often as she moved from room to room, he followed, but only to sit again when she stopped— a sleek statue of a cat with his long tail coiled around his feet, watching every move she made with his bronze-green eyes.

"What are you looking at?" Jessica yelled at him sometimes, whirling to face him. "Why do you follow me around and stare at me? Why don't you go do cat things like chasing your tail?"

Worm's eyes would flicker, like light moving through the mossy gold of swamp water, and his ears, turning sideways, would slide farther back on his head.

"Why don't you do what people expect of you, like

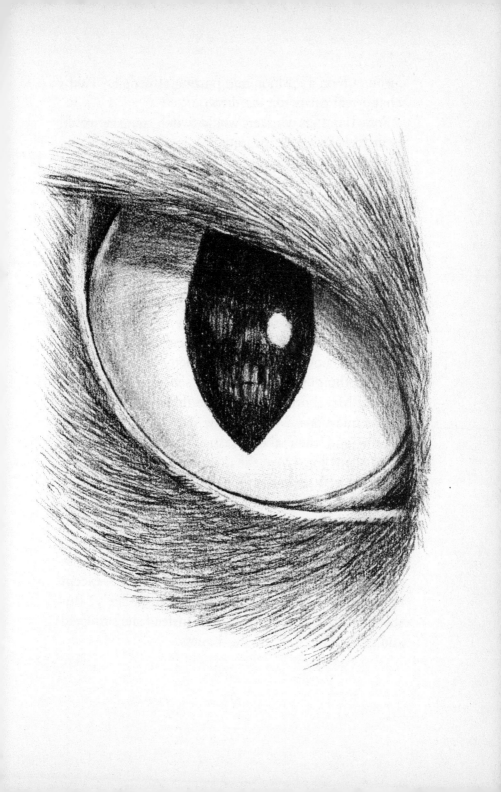

curling up on a cushion and purring at people? That's what a real cat is supposed to do."

Sometimes his whiskers would twitch, and she would seem to hear him answering. "A real cat?" he would say. "Why should I care what a real cat is supposed to do?"

During the fall months, while Worm was growing up, Mrs. Fortune continued to take a great interest in him and everything he did. From that first night when Jessica brought Worm home to her apartment, Mrs. Fortune went out of her way to question Jessica about him at every opportunity. It began to seem as if she really did have some weird way of knowing what was going on all over the apartment house, because no matter how quickly and quietly Jessica walked through the downstairs hallway, she was almost sure to meet Mrs. Fortune. And once they met, there were always questions. Mrs. Fortune would ask first about Worm, and then about Jessica, herself, and sometimes about Joy. Once she even asked about Brandon.

"Have you seen Brandon lately?" she asked. "He hasn't been to see me for quite a while."

Jessica happened to know, because she had overheard Joy talking to Mrs. Doyle on the telephone, that Brandon had been sick with the flu. Otherwise she wouldn't have known anything about him—except that he hadn't been playing his trumpet lately. But she didn't tell Mrs. Fortune that. Instead she shrugged and said, "He's had the flu, I guess."

"Ah, I thought it must be something like that."
Mrs. Fortune nodded her shaky old head so that it
seemed to be saying yes and no at the same time. "I
still bake molasses cookies every Tuesday," she said.
"Brandon usually comes to see me on Tuesdays."

Jessica sighed loudly, a bored, impatient sigh. "I
don't fool around with Brandon anymore. I don't
have the time, and besides—he bores me."

"Brandon bores you?" Mrs. Fortune said, incredu-
lous. Jessica knew it was a stupid thing to have said.
There were other complaints she could have made
about Brandon. She could have said he had a lot of
strange ideas, or that he had a violent temper, or
even that he was a stinking traitor who turned against
old friends for no reason—and that would have been
the truth. But no one in his right mind would believe
that Brandon had ever bored anyone.

But then, Mrs. Fortune wasn't in her right mind.
At least that's what a lot of people said. So Jessica
only stared at her and said, "Yeah, he bores me!"
Then she turned away and walked off, leaving Mrs.
Fortune standing there with her silly cats winding
around her feet.

One of the things Mrs. Fortune always said when
she met Jessica was that she should bring her cat
down for a visit, but Jessica never did. Then one day
Worm paid a visit to Mrs. Fortune, or at least to her
cats, all by himself.

It happened when Joy, hurrying out because she

was late for work, neglected to close the front door of the apartment. By the time Jessica discovered the slightly open door, Worm was nowhere to be found. She hurried out, searching everywhere, telling herself that Joy had probably done it on purpose because she hated Worm. Jessica searched all three floors, frantically looking in every possible hiding place, when she remembered the cat door and realized that Worm could have gone out into the back yard. She dashed out into the yard and found him there, watching a huddled bunch of Mrs. Fortune's cats.

The fence around the back yard of the Regency Apartment House was high and cat-proofed by an inward curved section of chicken wire at the top. Twice every day Mrs. Fortune let her cats out to sun themselves in the yard. Apparently the Fortune cats had been on one of their outings when Worm escaped and found his way out through the cat door. When Jessica arrived, all five of the fat old cats were crowded into a corner of the fence with their long fluffy tails bushed out and their eyes as big and round as nickels. A few feet away Worm sat, a slick and silent statue. His ears were turned sideways and his eyes were as cold and golden as the eyes of a crocodile.

Because she was curious, Jessica decided not to interfere, at least for a moment. She watched, wondering what all those cats—any one of whom outweighed Worm by twice at least—were so desperately afraid of, when close behind her a voice like a creaky hinge said, "Well, well, children. I see you have a visitor."

At the sound of Mrs. Fortune's voice, Worm stood, and with a slash of his tail, moved away to the other side of the yard. The other cats came out of the corner with a rush and wound themselves around Mrs. Fortune's feet, yowling up at her in pitiful complaining voices. While she made comforting noises at her crying cats, she kept her eyes on Worm as he paced deliberately away to the farthest fence. Finally she said, "You must have given him very good care, Jessica. He is large for his age. What is his name?"

Mrs. Fortune had asked before about his name, and Jessica had said he didn't have one. But now she said, "His name is Worm."

Mrs. Fortune's cats all had fancy and dignified names, like Lucasta and Ophelia and Simeon; but she didn't seem as surprised as Jessica expected about Worm's name. Her smile never unwrinkled and her head went on nodding and shaking at the same time. "Worm," she said. "Ah, yes. His name is Worm."

"My mother named him, actually," Jessica went on. "She said he looked like one when I first found him."

"Ah, yes, he was quite strange. Quite an unusual kitten."

"He's still unusual," Jessica said.

"Unusual? In what way is he unusual?"

"Well, for one thing, why are your cats afraid of him? They're all a lot bigger than he is."

Mrs. Fortune laughed fondly. "Well, I'm afraid my

51

poor kitties are just too old to face new things easily. Even half-grown kittens. They've led a very sheltered existence."

Although Jessica had often argued with Joy, insisting that Worm was a perfectly normal cat, she suddenly realized that she had known all along he was not. And now it made her angry that Mrs. Fortune would not admit it. "How about the way he looks?" she insisted angrily. "He doesn't look like any cat I've ever seen before."

"He is rather different looking. The shading and ears are like a rare breed I saw a few times, years ago, at cat shows, Abyssinians, I believe they were called. They're supposed to be descended from the cats of ancient Egypt, if I remember correctly."

Jessica might have had more to say about Worm, but by then the five old cats were yelling so loudly it was difficult to make herself heard. As soon as Mrs. Fortune turned toward the apartment house, they hushed and trotted ahead of her to the back door. After they were gone, Jessica picked up Worm and carried him back to the third floor.

As she stepped inside her apartment, Worm twisted out of her arms and dashed across the room to the window that looked down into the back yard. Leaping up to the windowsill, he stared down. Coming up behind him, Jessica could see that he was staring at the corner where he had held the Fortune cats prisoner. The end of his tail twitched spasmodically.

"There's no use watching for them," Jessica said. "They won't be out today anymore. They're probably so frightened they won't come out again for a week."

Worm's whiskers flickered, and Jessica thought he was saying, "They *should* be frightened."

A short time later, when Jessica was ready to leave for school, Worm was still sitting in the window, staring down at the corner of the yard.

"What's the matter with you?" Jessica asked. "Why do you hate them so much?"

Worm ignored her completely. Not even an ear moved in her direction as he continued to watch for the white cats.

"Look at me!" Jessica demanded with no result. Then she jumped at him suddenly, clapping her hands and making a loud noise.

"Ssssst!" she went, almost in his ear.

His reaction was not at all what she had expected. She had only meant to scare him to make him notice her, but instead of jumping and running away, he whirled to face her, and Jessica caught her breath in surprise—almost fear.

He looked so incredibly evil. His large pointed ears were twisted outward and shifted back on the sides of his head until they formed a horned crescent—like the horns of a devil. The long tufts of pale hair at their tips quivered in the light like thin blades of electric fire, and the pupils of his mossy golden eyes had narrowed to slits of darkness.

Jessica's breath escaped in a soft round "Oh" of surprise. "You really look like a devil," she said. A shiver prickled down her back as something vaguely frightening flickered and then died like a dark flame in a corner of her mind.

She shrugged and tried a scornful laugh. "But all you are really, is just some weird breed of cat. Mrs. Fortune said an Abyssinian, or something."

Worm's answer echoed strangely in her head, but she had imagined his responses for so long that she was almost out the door before the difference registered in her mind. Then she stopped as if she had been snapped up at the end of a rope.

"Mrs. Fortune knows more than she tells," Worm had said, and Jessica had *not* known that he was going to say it.

"He said that. He really said that. It wasn't me," she whispered.

She turned slowly, with dread and anticipation, and went back into the room.

# *Chapter Five*

WORM WAS STILL ON THE WINDOWSILL—BUT LYING now, with his front paws curled inward and his tail neatly coiled around him. He looked up at Jessica as she came toward him and yawned, showing a curl of pink tongue between sharp white teeth. When she squatted in front of him, staring intently, he simply stared back through sleepy hooded eyes.

"What did you say—about Mrs. Fortune?" Jessica asked. The only response was a sudden sharp twitch of the very tip of the soot-gray tail. She asked the question again, and then again louder, but Worm just watched her in sulky silence. Finally, she almost shouted into his ear, "What did you say? I know you said it!"

He got up slowly, then, and jumped down from the

window. Jessica followed him into the kitchen. He went directly to his food dish, sniffed it, and looked up at Jessica expectantly. It was a very ordinary cat-like thing to do, as if he'd decided not to give away his secret after all. She watched him, crouching over his raw liver and growling softly to himself, until it was very late and she had to run all the way to school.

From time to time during her classes, Jessica found her thoughts going back to Worm and what she had heard him say. Sometimes she was sure he had said it, and other times she wasn't. She had been imagining conversations between them for so long that it seemed likely she had only imagined again—automatically, without knowing she was doing it. Yet this had been different. This time the words had not come from anything that was already in her mind. They had come from someplace else—but from where, and how?

She tried to remember exactly how it had happened. Had she been looking directly at Worm when she heard it? She thought she had been and his narrow cat face had not moved in any way, except for the flow of green-gold light in his strange angry eyes. Then how had she heard it? With her ears? She didn't think so. It was more as if the words had suddenly happened, inside her head. And yet she could almost remember the sound of the voice—hollow and throbbing like a distant howl. The sound came and went in her head all day, interrupting other voices, making her pay even less attention than usual to her teachers. It wasn't until she was on her way home that something happened important enough to make her forget about Worm entirely, at least for a little while.

She was passing the drugstore on Spencer Street when the door swung open and Diane and Brenda rushed out, giggling and chattering. They almost bumped into Jessica before they saw her.

"Oh, hi, Jessica," Diane said with phony enthusiasm.

Brenda said hello, too, but much more coolly. For a long time Jessica didn't say anything at all, while Diane fidgeted, smiling stupidly and stammering beginnings of things that she couldn't finish.

Finally Jessica said, "Big surprise. I thought you walked home on Grant Street now."

"Well I do, usually. Because of my mother. That is, my mother said I had to because the traffic is better. I mean it's worse on Spencer, and that little kid got hit here last year and everything. But we came this way today because Brenda had to get something at the drugstore."

Jessica looked at Diane, letting her see that she didn't believe that stuff about her mother. If Diane walked home on Grant now, it was because Jessica always walked up Spencer. And if Diane was embarrassed to see Jessica since she'd dropped her for a fat slob with a swimming pool, she ought to say so and not make up stupid lies about it.

"Look, Diane," Jessica said. "I *know* why you don't

walk home on Spencer anymore, and it doesn't make any difference to me. So you don't have to make up lies about it."

Diane's face crumpled completely. She had never been much good in an argument, at least not when anyone was really angry. "It's not a lie," she said. There was a jerkiness to her voice, as if she were starting to cry. "My mother *did* say I couldn't walk home on Spencer anymore. She drove past one day when I was outside of Dino's, and she got mad and said I was to stay off Spencer and if I didn't I'd be kept at home for a month."

Jessica shrugged and smiled in a way that let Diane see what she thought of that story. Brenda was glaring at Jessica furiously. Jessica had heard that redheads had horrible tempers. She wondered if that was what Brenda and Diane saw in each other. It took someone as mousy as Diane to get along with a really bad-tempered person like Brenda, even if she did have a swimming pool.

Brenda grabbed Diane's arm and pulled her away. Diane looked back uncertainly and said, "Good-by, Jessica," but she let herself be led up the sidewalk. As they walked off, Brenda was talking rapidly. Jessica couldn't hear much of it, but she was sure of one phrase. Brenda had been saying something about a "jealous witch."

All the way home those words pounded in Jessica's ears. "Jealous witch—jealous!" She'd show them she wasn't jealous of their stupid swimming-pool friendship. She didn't know how yet, but she'd find a way.

When she got home, she slammed the door and threw her books down on the coffee table; and it wasn't until that moment, when Worm slithered out from under the table, that she remembered again about the morning. Then she remembered with shocking force because, once more, Worm's ears were devil horns and his eyes hooded and evil.

In the middle of the floor, Worm stopped and sat, facing Jessica. With his long thin body erect and his tail tightly coiled around his haunches, he looked like a cat-god carved from stone. Jessica approached him slowly and sank to the floor in front of him. Sitting cross-legged, she stared back into his crocodile eyes.

"You look like a devil," she whispered, and almost immediately a sound stirred and swelled in her head. A strange wavering sound, part yowl and part speech. Each word rose and fell in volume, ending in a trailing wail. "You—look—like—a—jealous—witch," it said.

Jessica crossed her arms, pulling against a wild churning of emotions. Anger, surprise, and shock, but most of all an overwhelming rush of fierce and burning excitement—a bitter painful joy.

"They were lying," she gasped at last. "I'm not jealous of them. They lied about that. They're always lying about me. They lie about everything. Like not being allowed to walk on Spencer Street."

The sound came again—the words distant and hollow. "Perhaps that wasn't a lie," it said.

Jessica was trembling; she clutched herself harder to hold the trembling deep inside. "Perhaps," she whispered, because she was beginning to see. Diane had said her mother was angry when she found Diane outside of Dino's—and suddenly that sounded like the truth.

Dino's was a slot-machine place just two doors away from the drugstore. A lot of boys, older boys mostly, were always hanging around there. Diane liked to walk past Dino's. Even last year in seventh grade, she had liked to. Even then she had been developing a very noticeable figure; and having never been the least bit noticeable before, she was very interested in the way boys were beginning to pay attention. Jessica remembered that now. And she also remembered Diane's mother. Mrs. Darby was the kind who made Diane polish her white shoes every single morning. She was even fussier about certain other things. The part of the story about Dino's just could have been the truth.

Jessica stared at the burning gold of Worm's eyes and listened—and the howl in her head said, "You could make sure. You could find out if it was a lie."

Jessica nodded. She stood up and walked slowly to the telephone. With her hand on the phone, she thought for a long time before she dialed. Then waiting for someone to answer, she made her eyes wide and friendly and pitched her voice to match.

"Hello," she said when Diane's mother came on. "Is Diane there?"

"No, she isn't," Diane's mother said. "May I take a message?"

"Well, this is Jessica."

"Well, hello, Jessica." Mrs. Darby sounded surprised. "We haven't seen you here for quite a while. Where have you been?"

"Oh, I've been very busy lately, Mrs. Darby," Jessica said.

"Well, we've missed you. Diane is at Brenda's house this afternoon. Would you like to call her there?"

"Well, maybe I will. But in case I can't get her there, could you give her a message?"

"Certainly."

"Okay. Fine. Would you just ask her if she knows what happened to my new fountain pen? See, on the way home from school today, out in front of—— I mean, it was when I was walking home from school, I happened to see Diane and she borrowed my fountain pen. She needed it to write down a phone number or something. And then someone else borrowed it to write a phone number, and I never got it back. And it was a new one I just bought."

"Where did you say you were when you saw Diane?" Mrs. Darby said in a tight voice.

"Well, I didn't say, exactly. It was just on the way home. She was with Brenda."

There was a pause before Diane's mother said, "Jessica, I really must insist that you tell me where Diane was when you saw her this afternoon."

"I can't, Mrs. Darby," Jessica said. "I can't get Diane in trouble when she's such a good friend of mine, and everything."

"I'm quite certain that I already know where Diane was when she borrowed your pen," Mrs. Darby said. "So you might as well tell me all about it. I promise I won't say anything to Diane about where I found out."

"Won't you?" Jessica said. "Do you really promise —because I'd just about kill myself if Diane got mad at me."

After Mrs. Darby promised and repromised not to tell how she'd found out, Jessica told her that she'd met Diane and Brenda on Spencer Street, near the drugstore.

"Near what store?" Mrs. Darby asked.

"Well, it was pretty near the drugstore."

"I suppose you mean she was in front of that penny-arcade place, Dino's I believe it's called?"

"I guess it wasn't too far from there?"

"What was Diane doing there?"

"Nothing. Nothing at all, Mrs. Darby. She was just talking to—uh—some other kids. I think they're friends of Brenda's. And this one—uh, person—wanted to know Diane's phone number, and that's how I happened to lend her my pen."

When the conversation was over, Jessica went on sitting by the phone for a while, thinking and planning. Important ideas kept flashing into her mind. It occurred to her that it would be wise to call back soon and say she'd found the fountain pen. Then Mrs. Darby wouldn't have to mention it to Diane. And later in the evening, maybe even quite late at night, she could call and not say anything when Mr. or Mrs. Darby answered the phone, as if someone wanted to talk to Diane who definitely *didn't* want to talk to her parents. Knowing Diane's parents, Jessica could easily imagine what would happen at the Darby house that night. She could easily predict that it would be at least a month before Diane would have another chance to swim in Brenda's fancy swimming pool—or to do much of anything else, for that matter.

When Jessica was finally finished at the telephone, Worm was no longer sitting in the middle of the floor. She looked in all his usual hideouts before she found him at last, curled up at the back of her closet. She pulled him out and put him in the middle of the floor, but he refused to speak, or even to pay attention. Turning away from Jessica he collapsed limply on the floor.

"You know what I did, don't you?" she asked him, but he just flicked a narrow glance in her direction and began to lick the soft inward curve of a paw, where the claws lay hidden in gray velvet.

"It wasn't my idea," Jessica said, but Worm went

on washing. She sat down near him then and pounded on the floor with both fists. Worm leaped to his feet, with curved back and flattened ears. Jessica grinned angrily. "See," she said. "Stop pretending. Stop pretending you're just a cat."

That night very late, Jessica awoke feeling hot and heavy. The blankets seemed tight and twisted, and the darkness pressed down on her chest like a weight. No matter how she turned and struggled, she couldn't get comfortable, and pictures kept forming in the darkness behind her eyes.

The pictures flowed and changed, blending into dreams as, now and then, she sank briefly into restless sleep. Diane and Brenda, walking up Spencer Street together, melted into a dream in which Diane, flattened into a gigantic paper doll, with her pretty round-eyed face torn and crumpled, drifted behind Brenda.

The dream dissolved, and Jessica awoke to stare into darkness until sleep came again. But with it came another dream—an old familiar one. It had been years since she had dreamt it, but nothing had changed. It was as it had always been, clear and sharp in detail, and full of an incredible intangible terror.

She seemed to be waking from a deep sleep, but instead of being in her own bed, she was lying on a small white cot that sat in the very middle of a small room. Except for the bed, the room was completely empty and bare, with no furniture or pictures, not even a window. The walls and ceiling and floor were all

the same—a nameless nothing color—too dull to be white, but not so deep as gray. As Jessica lay motionless, already terrified without yet knowing why, she began to feel the bed shrinking beneath her, while all around the pale walls began to expand, moving outward and away. She reached out, trying desperately to grasp something, but it was too late—there was nothing there. At last everything was gone. Everything, memory and thought and finally even fear, and she was left floating in the middle of a nothingness that went on and on forever.

Jessica awoke wet with sweat and sat up in bed. Then, just as she had always done when the dream came, she slipped out of bed and crept noiselessly down the hall. The door to Joy's room opened without a sound, and the light from Jessica's room, seeping down the hallway, was enough to show that Joy was there—a lump under the covers, her blond hair spread out on the pillow. When she was sure, Jessica went back and crawled into bed.

# Chapter Six

AT LAST IT WAS MORNING, AND THE ALARM CLOCK'S jarring clamor put an end to both sleep and dreams. Jessica got up quickly and had the coffee on and the table set before Joy appeared, puffy-eyed and tousled.

"Well," Joy said, when she noticed what Jessica had done. "What's this? What have you done now?"

"What do you mean, what have I done now?"

"You know what I mean. Every time you start getting useful, it turns out I'm about to get some unpleasant news. Like an *F* in math or a broken window. What have you been up to this time?"

"I—haven't—done—anything," Jessica said very slowly and distinctly. "I just wanted to talk to you. I just thought if I helped, you might have time to talk to me before you left for work."

The eggs and toast were on the table before anyone broke the angry silence. At last Joy sighed and said, "I'm sorry, Jessie. I shouldn't have said that." She smiled a lop-sided smile and blinked her long eyelashes. "You know how grumpy I am until I've had my coffee." She glanced at her watch. "What did you want to talk to me about?"

"Nothing," Jessica said.

"No, tell me," Joy said. "I want to know."

"Nothing," Jessica said. "I didn't want to talk about anything." She got up from the table, clattered her dishes into the sink, and went to her room. Locking the door behind her, she sat down on the bed.

A few minutes later, Joy's hurrying footsteps stopped at Jessica's door. "Jessie," she said, trying the doorknob.

Jessica sat perfectly still. "Jessie!" Joy said louder. "Open this door." Finally she yelled, "Brat!" And her footsteps went angrily down the hall and out the front door.

Jessica lay on the bed, thinking. It was just as well, she decided, that she hadn't tried to tell Joy about what had happened. Joy would never have believed it about Worm. She would have laughed, probably, the way she'd laughed once when she saw Jessica and Brandon doing one of their book plays. Or, even worse, she might have taken it seriously, too seriously. She might have sent Jessica to a psychiatrist again.

Joy had sent Jessica to a psychiatrist once, when the first-grade teacher had complained that Jessica slept all day in class. The psychiatrist had been a very smart man; he had figured out right away that Jessica slept all day in school because she didn't sleep at night. But he wasn't smart enough to find out why. Jessica had decided she didn't want anyone to know about the empty-room dream, so she had made up a story about being afraid of a monster who sometimes hid in her closet. The psychiatrist had made Joy stay home every night and come into Jessica's room over and over again to show her that the closet was empty. After a while, Jessica got better at sleeping, except when Joy was out, and Joy had quit sending her to the psychiatrist.

But whether she laughed or sent for a psychiatrist, Joy would certainly never have believed, for even a moment, that Worm had really talked to Jessica. The thing was, Jessica was not really sure of it herself. Perhaps she'd only imagined it.

She might very well have imagined it; and if she had, she knew why—and what had caused it. All those years that she'd spent playing those crazy games with Brandon—games where you had to imagine all kinds of crazy things—had gotten her so much into the habit that she wasn't able to tell, sometimes, whether she was imagining or not.

That must have been it. She'd imagined it all—and it wasn't her fault or Worm's fault either. It was Brandon's fault for teaching her to have such a crazy imagination.

Jessica realized, suddenly, that she had been lying

on her bed thinking for a long time and she was almost late for school. She jumped up, grabbed her books and coat, and was opening the door to her room when suddenly she stopped. Worm usually stayed hidden until Joy left for work, but he would be out by now, prowling around the apartment.

Without asking herself why she didn't want to see him, Jessica opened the door a crack and peeked around it. He was not in the hallway. Hastily she tiptoed to the door of the living room and eased through it. He must be in the kitchen, eating his breakfast, she thought and hurried across the room, glancing back over her shoulder at the kitchen door. She was already in the tiny entry hall before she saw him. He was sitting in front of the door, a tall tapering pillar of a cat, entwined by a snakelike tail.

Jessica's heart thudded, and she caught her breath, but then she laughed disgustedly—at herself mostly, for being so ridiculous.

"Sssst," she said. "Scat! Get out of my way."

Worm stood up slowly, and with slashing tail, moved slowly and deliberately around Jessica, across the living room and into the kitchen. Jessica watched until he was out of sight, and then she slipped out the door and slammed it behind her.

"See," she told herself. "He didn't say anything. Not a word. I knew he wouldn't."

And yet later, that very day, she found herself saying, "I'll tell Worm. I'll tell him it worked." It happened when school was over and Jessica was on her way out of the school building. She looked toward the street and there were Brenda and Diane, standing by the curb. Brenda was talking, nodding her head and making sharp angry gestures, while Diane stood with her head down, saying very little. From time to time, she shook her head. Then a car approached the curb, and she gave Brenda a quick little shove and walked away.

Diane got into the car without looking back or waving to Brenda, and Mrs. Darby, who was at the wheel, didn't wave either. Brenda waved though, hard and defiantly, until the car was out of sight.

Jessica walked the other way, across the yard, feeling nothing at first except a kind of numbness that was almost like surprise. But then suddenly she walked faster, prodded by a sharp twinge of that fierce excitement. And that was when she found herself saying, "I'll tell Worm. I'll tell him it worked."

During the next few days, Jessica told Worm how well the fountain-pen story had worked, not just once, but many times. She told him how glad she was that it had worked because it served them right. It served Diane right for trading a friendship for a crummy swimming pool, and Brenda for being spoiled and conceited and for stealing other people's friends. It served them both right, and most of the time Jessica was sure she was glad about it. Anyway, it was done, and no one could change anything now.

71

As for Worm, Jessica didn't know what to think. Sometimes she told Worm that he was just an ordinary, stupid cat, and she knew perfectly well that he had never said anything to anybody and never would. At other times she wasn't sure. But no matter what she said to him, Worm only watched her silently through slitted eyes.

The rest of that week crept by so slowly it seemed as if it were never going to end. School, which for some time had been getting more and more impossible, became even worse. Jessica spent hours of class time thinking about Worm and other things. At last the school week ended, but the weekend was no better, and Sunday was the worst of all.

Joy left early in the afternoon for a ride in the country and a dinner date with Alan; and after a long boring day, Jessica had only hours and hours of reading or TV—and Mrs. Post's visit—to look forward to. She had read for a long time when she began to feel hungry and decided to fix herself something to eat.

It was while she was on her way to the kitchen that she noticed Worm, sitting on the windowsill, halfway hidden by the drape. He was staring down into the back yard so intently that Jessica stopped and looked, too.

Enormous floodlights made the back yard almost as bright as day. Frank, Mrs. Post's husband, had installed them to illuminate the murderers his wife was

72

always looking for. But Jessica guessed that Worm was looking for something besides murderers.

"They aren't there," she told him. "She never lets them out this late at night. You're imagining things."

But Worm only went on staring, his tail twitching in sharp angry flicks. His ears were moving, too, shifting backwards, stretching his eyes into sharper diamonds. Jessica caught her breath as excitement welled up, swift and hot, drowning her first brief impulse to turn quickly away and hurry on to the kitchen. She crouched by the windowsill, bringing her face close to Worm's.

"Say something," she said. "Say something! Like you did before. Say something, you stupid cat!"

Worm's evil, angry face was turning toward her, and Jessica could feel the excitement growing and spreading, when suddenly his ears twitched and flicked forward. He leaped down from the sill and slid, a flowing gray shadow, beneath the overstuffed chair. At the same instant, there was the familiar creaking of the stairs, and a moment later a knock on the front door.

Jessica stood up slowly, breathing hard, her fists clenched at her sides. She waited until Mrs. Post had knocked twice before she yelled, "Come in." She stayed at the window with her back to the room as Mrs. Post puffed across to her favorite chair and sighed slowly into it.

"Jessica," she whined. "You still aren't remembering to lock the door. I've talked to your mother about it, and she agrees with me that you really must be more careful. You really must remember to lock the door whenever you're here alone. Didn't you read in the paper this very morning about what happened to that poor woman in the Parkwood Apartments? And that's not such a long way——"

Mrs. Post's voice trailed off for a moment and then rose again like the whine of an electric saw. "What are you doing there in the window, Jessica? What is it? What are you looking at?" The tone sharpened as if the saw had struck a nail. "Is there someone in the back yard?"

A sound moved through the angry fumes in Jessica's mind. "A man," it howled. "There was a man in the yard."

"There was a man in the yard," Jessica said. "He was sneaking along by the fence, and he had something tied across his face."

Almost immediately, Mrs. Post was behind her, smothering her against the window frame as she peered out into the yard. Her soft bulges pressed around Jessica, smelling of disinfectant and stale lilac powder.

"Where?" she said. "Where is he? Lord help us. Where is he? I told Frank this was going to happen. Where is he, Jessica? I don't see anyone."

"He's gone," Jessica said. "He went in the back door into the downstairs hall."

"Ohhh!" Mrs. Post made a noise like a stepped-on rubber squeak-toy and moving faster than Jessica would ever have imagined she could, she dashed to the telephone and began to dial. "Ohh, ohh," she squeaked with every number. Then she stopped dialing and only moaned while she waited for the phone to be answered. It must have rung several times before she whispered, "Hello, hello, Frank, is that you?" There was a pause and then she rushed on in a frantic whimper. "Frank, there's a man down there—in the hall. He went in just a minute ago—through the back door. No, just now—just a minute before I called. You were? For how long? Well, no, but Jessica did. Well, just a moment. I'll be right down."

Mrs. Post hung up the phone and surged out the door, calling back for Jessica to be sure to turn the lock. Jessica did, and then immediately ran back and dropped to her knees beside the overstuffed chair, but Worm was not there. Sometime during the phoning he must have crept out of the room. Jessica looked in most of his usual hiding places before she found him in her bedroom, sitting in the middle of her bed. As she came in, he began to wash his face, licking a paw and scrubbing behind his ear and down his face, but all the time watching Jessica through the cracks of his slitted eyes.

Jessica laughed harshly, and the angry excitement burned higher as she sank down beside the bed, bringing her face close to Worm's.

75

"All right," she said. "You can stop pretending. You can stop acting like an ordinary cat. I heard you. I heard you say there was a man in the yard."

Worm had stopped washing, but his face remained blank and innocently owllike. He stared at Jessica with eyes whose pupils, in the dim light of the bedroom, had grown to enormous black holes.

"We really scared old Post," Jessica said excitedly. She bugged her eyes, pitched her voice to "electric-whine," and said, "Where is he? I knew it. I knew this was going to happen." She laughed again at her own impersonation. "She's probably down there right now telling Frank 'I told you so.' She's always fussing at him about robbers and murderers and making him put double locks on everything, and he always just laughs at her. So now she's down there saying 'I told you so!'"

There was a loud sharp knock on the door, and Jessica jumped to her feet, startled and immediately apprehensive. "Something's gone wrong," she said.

Glaring at Worm, she said, "You'd better help me. It's all your fault." But he only went on staring out of empty black holes, rimmed with gold.

"All right!" Jessica hissed. "All right for you!" And she ran to unlock the door.

It was Mrs. Post again, only redder in the face and puffing more than ever. But instead of making for her favorite chair, she only stood heaving and glaring, while Jessica felt herself getting more and more tense and frightened. At last, in an ominously quiet voice, Mrs. Post said, "Jessica. Why did you lie to me? Why did you lie about seeing someone in the yard?"

Jessica tried not to let herself show the fright that made the skin of her face feel tight and crawly.

"Lie?" she said. "I didn't lie. What did I say that was a lie?"

Mrs. Post shook her head slowly. "Jessica. I *know* you were lying about seeing someone in the back yard and about seeing him go into the building. No one came into the building."

"He did!" Jessica said. "He did, too. He must have run through the hall and out the front door before Mr. Post had time to look for him. There was plenty of time for him to run out the front door."

There was a long pause while Mrs. Post stared, her eyes hot and angry in her red face. The anger grew, stretching and swelling, until Jessica felt as if a gigantic balloon was about to explode in front of her.

"No, Jessica," Mrs. Post squeezed out through lips held tight against the explosion. "Mr. Post had been standing outside the door to Mrs. Fortune's apartment for at least fifteen minutes before I called. He'd gone to check the doors, and he met Mrs. Fortune in the hall, they'd been standing there talking—just a few feet from the back door—right up until I called. That's why it took him so long to answer the phone. I don't know why you lied to me, Jessica, but I'm certainly going to tell your mother in the morning."

To be caught, so inescapably caught, was so shattering that for a moment Jessica felt terrified—lost and hopeless. She backed away, putting her hands up in front of her face, palms outward. She had done that for years, whenever she was badly frightened. When she was very small, she had often awakened with her hands before her eyes—to ward off the terror of the dream about the empty room. But it had been a long time since she had done it where anyone could see.

At the moment she realized what she was doing, Jessica caught a glimpse of Mrs. Post's face. It was only a fleeting impression, but it was enough to tell her that something was changing. The angry flush was fading from the wide face as it clouded over with curiosity and concern.

"What is it, Jessica?" Mrs. Post asked.

Jessica let her hands remain where they were and her face crumpled as if with pain. Through half-shut eyes she checked the effect on Mrs. Post, and the results were encouraging. Mrs. Post was obviously fascinated. Jessica's hands came down very slowly while her face went blank and bewildered. She looked around in a dazed way and then rubbed her forehead.

"I—I feel so funny," she faltered. "Dizzy—I can't seem to think straight. Is—is it late? Is my mother home?"

"No, she's not home," Mrs. Post said. "But I think she should be. Do you know where to call her?"

Jessica shook her head slowly. "No, I don't. I think

she told me, but I can't remember. I can't seem to remember—anything."

Mrs. Post was looking more and more concerned. She put her hand on Jessica's forehead. "I think you may have a fever," she said. "A fever can make a person's mind do strange things sometimes. You really should be in bed, Jessica. Let me help you get into bed. You're probably just coming down with the flu."

Without saying or doing anything more, except that she went on acting a little vague and confused, Jessica allowed herself to be put to bed. But even after she was tucked under the covers, Mrs. Post did not leave. She moved her favorite chair into the bedroom and sat there until Jessica finally pretended to be sound asleep. Then Mrs. Post got up, and Jessica heard her floppy slippers scuffling their way to the front door and creaking down the stairs. Immediately, Jessica jumped out of bed and went looking for Worm.

Worm was hiding again, and as Jessica looked and looked, she got more and more angry. She finally found him in Joy's room, where he seldom went. He was far back under the bed, and she reached under and pulled him out by one hind leg. He spit and yowled and dug his claws into the rug, but she jerked him loose and carried him roughly into the living room. When she dropped him in the middle of the floor, he struck at her as he fell, raking the air near her hand with a claw-fringed paw.

Jessica laughed angrily. She squatted in front of Worm, ready to jump away if he moved toward her. For a long moment he poised, humpbacked and bristling—like a Halloween cat on the end of a flying broom. Then, slowly, he sank to his haunches, and Jessica sat, too, and waited.

"Look what you've done now," she said at last. "Look what you've gotten me into."

Worm stared back, owl-faced, shallow-eyed, and silent, until Jessica leaned forward sharply and hissed, "See! See what you did!"

His ears flattened then and suddenly his eyes were flowing with brassy fire. Jessica felt the hot flare of excitement even before the howl began.

"I see. I seee——" The voice rose and fell throbbingly. "I see that you frightened her and she deserved it, and you are not in trouble."

"Not in trouble?" Jessica said. "She'll tell that I lied about seeing a man. And it was your idea. You told me to say there was a man in the yard. I was mad at her for barging in, but I wouldn't have thought about saying I saw a man. It was your idea."

There was a silence that lasted until Jessica began to think there was no more to come; but at last the voice began again—distant and indistinct at first, then growing louder. "She is not angry. She is no longer angry. No one will be. They will think you are innocent."

"Innocent? But she knows I lied."

"Yes, she knows. But she thinks you could not help it—that you are innocent."

Through a long frozen silence, Jessica sat staring into the burning gold of Worm's eyes, until a deepening cold made her shiver violently.

"You're evil," she said. "You are——"

"A witch's cat." The voice was fainter now, but what it said was unmistakable. In a hollow moan that rose almost to a wail and then throbbed away into silence, it said, "I am a witch's cat."

Jessica hunched her shoulders against another shudder. For a long time, she sat very still, trying to untangle strange dark images from reasonable ideas and arguments.

"A witch's cat?" she whispered at last. "You can't be a witch's cat. What witch? When were you a witch's cat?"

No answer. Jessica waited and watched until she saw that Worm's ears had cupped forward and his eyes were rounding into blank metallic disks. He stood then, stretched, and stalked away, glancing back only once at Jessica. As he turned away, he slashed the air with his long tail as if daring her to try to stop him.

Jessica didn't try. She sat stiffly instead, feeling the excitement burning lower and lower until it faded into something cold and gray and unpleasant. The cold went with her when she went back to bed.

The extra blankets she piled on her bed were heavy, and she soon felt hot and smothery; but when she threw the blankets off, she found herself shivering in a chill cocoon of sheets. Time passed slowly, and at last she heard Joy arriving home, pausing briefly in the doorway of the room while Jessica, as always, pretended to be asleep. Long after Joy had gone to bed, Jessica was still awake.

She lay stiffly with eyes as wide as broken windows —so open and empty that the darkness seemed to spill through into her mind. Thoughts and ideas that might have seemed impossible by daylight moved freely and tangibly in the darkness, growing and changing into new and strange convictions.

"A witch's cat," she thought. "Of course. That explains it. That explains the voice—and the things it tells me to do. But who is the witch? And why did she send him here—to me?"

At breakfast the next morning, Joy was her usual self, too rushed and distracted to say more than a brief good-morning. Obviously Mrs. Post hadn't had a chance to tell about what had happened the night before. But she would tell, as soon as she got the chance. There was no doubt about that.

The moment Joy left the apartment, Jessica hurried to her room for her things and from there to the front door. She would be very early for school, but it couldn't be helped. She could not stay alone in the apartment any longer.

At the door she turned to look back. Worm would be emerging soon from wherever he'd hidden himself, and she didn't want to see him. At least not right away. Before Worm had a chance to talk to her again, there were some things she had to know.

# Chapter Seven

THAT DAY, THE DAY AFTER THE SCARING OF MRS. Post, Jessica stopped at the library on the way home from school. There she discovered that the book she had lost the night she found Worm still had not been replaced. The librarian said that after they'd given up on Jessica's book, they had ordered another copy, but it had never arrived. "I don't understand why," the librarian said. "There's been plenty of time. Are you particularly interested in the Salem witch trials? Perhaps we have some other material on them."

"Well, I guess so," Jessica said. "About witches. I just thought I'd like to read some stuff about witches."

The librarian smiled. "That seems to be a very popular subject lately," she said. "Witches and ghosts and all kinds of magic. It seems to be a real fad.

Nearly everything we have is out, but I'll see what's still on the shelves."

Jessica took the only two books she could get, old ones with faded frazzled covers and many pages of small dark print. She could hardly wait to start reading. Surely in all those pages there would be some answers—though she was not yet certain just what all the questions were.

However, the questions and the answers, too, had to wait, because when Jessica got home she discovered that Mrs. Post had told on her. Mrs. Post had called Joy at work and asked her to come home early for a very important conference about Jessica. She had refused to go into it any further on the phone and had hung up, leaving Joy to imagine all sorts of horrible things all day. Then when Joy got home, Mrs. Post had told her everything that had happened. Apparently she had made a big thing out of the way Jessica had acted, and had kept insisting that Jessica showed "distinct signs of emotional disturbance."

So Jessica was almost in trouble. She would have been in trouble, for sure and certain, if it had not been for the way Joy felt about Mrs. Post. Joy had always said that Mrs. Post was a fat old busybody and a gloom merchant, who just loved to exaggerate anything the least bit unpleasant. Furthermore, Mrs. Post had never approved of Joy and had never lost an opportunity to lecture her, particularly about the way she was rearing Jessica.

86

"She's too old and fat to have a good time herself, so she just can't stand to see somebody else enjoying life a little," Joy always said. "That's the only reason she insists on dragging herself up here to check on you every time I go out. I keep telling her it isn't necessary, but she keeps doing it just to make me feel guilty. I always let her know when I'm going to be out, in case of an emergency, but you don't really need for her to come clear up to the third floor to check on you, do you, Jessie?"

"I hate it," Jessica said. "She always snoops around and says things about how *her* kids were raised—as if nobody does it right anymore. And she always says things about how much you go out."

"See," Joy said. "That's exactly what I mean. She just loves to make people feel guilty. And I came close to telling her so, too. But I didn't. I just told her that you undoubtedly *thought* you saw a man in the yard, and that every kid who is a little bit unusual and original isn't necessarily emotionally disturbed. That's exactly what I told her. And the next time I see her, I'm going to tell her that there's no reason for her to come up here all the time, sticking her nose into our affairs. That's exactly what I'm going to tell her."

So, as it turned out, Jessica actually wasn't in very much trouble. However, the whole thing was very time-consuming. Joy talked for a long, long time. For the first hour or so she talked about how Mrs. Post had frightened her for no good reason and how unimportant and ridiculous the whole thing was. Then, in the next hour, she started changing her mind. After she had fixed herself a couple of strong drinks, because, she said, she really needed them after Mrs. Post, she began to wonder if Mrs. Post could have been right, after all.

When Joy began to wipe her eyes and talk about how she hadn't been a very good mother, Jessica went out into the kitchen to begin dinner; and that was the end of it. After dinner, they didn't talk about it anymore.

It wasn't until she was in bed that night that Jessica got around to the books on magic and witchcraft. She found both of them extremely interesting, though neither seemed to be exactly what she was looking for —that is, they didn't really seem to help her with Worm.

They were not easy books to read. The print was very small, and the sentences were long and complicated with many unfamiliar words. The first one was a history of witchcraft—descriptions of the times and places where people believed in witches. It told how witches all over the world had been accused and tried and punished. The trials at Salem were mentioned, but there was no information given that Jessica did not already have. After skimming most of the book, Jessica decided to try the other one before settling down to read more carefully.

The second book was even more difficult to read,

but at the same time more fascinating. In strange stilted language it told about many weird and terrible events. There were several stories about famous haunted houses. There was one about a fog-en-shrouded hollow on a country road where several people disappeared and were never seen again. And there was one about a young woman who was possessed by a demon.

It was very late, past two o'clock in the morning, when Jessica began the chapter about the demon. The first pages told how a young girl had made an insulting remark to a strange old woman who lived in a deserted barn on the edge of town. On the next day, a large black dog had appeared on the doorstep of the young woman's home and had refused to go away. Immediately afterward, the girl had begun to act strangely and to talk to people whom no one else could see.

Jessica was reading rapidly, with a feeling of rising excitement, when a sudden sound broke the deep early-morning stillness. Dropping the book, she sank down beneath the covers until she could barely peer out. The only light in the room was the small reading lamp by the bed. Outside its narrow radius, mysterious shadows swarmed out and away from the dark side of every object. Jessica's eyes darted from corner to corner until the noise came again, and the door, which had been slightly ajar, began to move slowly inward. Staring in breathless horror, Jessica watched while the door inched forward and then stopped, and near the floor a dark shape emerged from behind it.

The breath she'd been holding escaped in an angry hiss as Jessica recognized the narrow head and sleek pointed face. "Get out," she said. "Get out of my room and stay out." But Worm stayed where he was until Jessica snatched up the book she had been reading and threw it at him as hard as she could.

She'd never been able to throw straight when she was angry—rocks or clods or books never hit the right person—and this time was no exception. The book curved away from Worm and hit a metal wastepaper basket with a terrible clang. Worm leaped back and disappeared, and a moment later Joy rushed into the room.

"What was that?" Joy asked. "What made that crashing noise?"

"It was just Worm, I guess," Jessica said. "He came in and knocked over my wastepaper basket."

Joy looked at the wastepaper basket—and the book lying beside it. Picking up the book, she glanced at the title, *Strange Tales of the Supernatural,* and began to leaf through it. She read a bit in several places, and as she read her frown darkened.

"What is this thing?" she said at last.

"Just a book," Jessica said. "I got it at the library."

"Well, no wonder you've been acting funny if this is the kind of junk you've been reading," Joy said. She noticed the other book on the bed table and picked it up, too. She put them both under her arm.

"I'm taking these back to the library tomorrow," she said. "And I'm going to have a talk with that librarian. She shouldn't let you take out stuff like this. Why, these aren't even from the children's section."

So the books on witches went back to the library, and the librarians were told not to let Jessica check out any more books on witchcraft. Which left Jessica knowing only a little about some things that she needed desperately to know a lot about.

The information she had gotten from the two books amounted only to parts and pieces—enough to shape some new questions, but not to reach answers. The only thing the books had made her sure of was that Worm had talked to her—and that he was certainly a demon, a witch's cat. She only wondered, now, how she could have doubted it for so long.

There had been so many clues, starting from that first night, when she had found him, and lost the book about the Salem witches. The most convincing clues were, of course, his strange uncatlike behavior: the way he never romped or played, the way he followed her, watching and waiting, when she was alone, and hid himself away when anyone else was around. And now there was something even more significant: the fact that he had crept into her room in the middle of the night and kept her from finishing the books that might have given her some answers.

With the books gone, and no way to get more, there was no place to go for information. A year before she would have talked to Brandon about it. There weren't many people she could talk to about such a strange problem, but Brandon would have been perfect. Not that he would have known all the answers, but at least he would have listened and believed. Remembering all the things that Brandon had believed in, Jessica was sure that he would have believed her about Worm.

The only other possibility was Mrs. Fortune, but Jessica didn't really consider telling her. She wasn't sure exactly why, but the very idea made her feel uneasy, almost frightened. "It would just be a waste of time," Jessica told herself. "She's too old and crazy to understand—and besides, she knows too much already."

Of course there was Worm himself. He had said that he was a witch's cat, and someday he might say more. Someday he might say who the witch was, and why he had been sent to Jessica. During the long afternoons when they were home alone together, Jessica began to watch him constantly, almost as constantly as Worm watched her. As he paced or sat, a silent gray shadow, Jessica turned to face him again and again. Sometimes, staring into the blank bronze eyes, she would breathe a question.

"Who are you?" she would ask, or, "Who sent you?" or, "Why were you sent to me?"; but there was no answer except for an occasional flicker in the cold golden eyes.

93

Jessica only dared to question Worm by daylight. When night came, she did not try. Of course, on the nights when Joy was at home, there was no opportunity, because Worm, as always, hid himself away. But on the other nights, the nights when Joy went out and Jessica was left alone in the apartment with the empty darkness pressing in from all around, she did not try to talk to Worm. She did not try because she was sure, terribly frighteningly sure, that he would answer.

The moment Joy went out the door, Jessica hurried into her bedroom and turned the key in the lock. She came out briefly, of course, when Mrs. Post made her inevitable appearance, but that was all. The rest of the evening she spent lying on her bed, reading or only waiting until she heard Joy's key in the front door. Sometimes lying there on her bed, she would see a silent shadow flicker in the crack below her door and her shoulders would twitch in a wrenching shudder.

"Go away, witch's cat," she would whisper. "Go away."

# Chapter Eight

JESSICA KNEW THAT JOY HAD NOT DONE WHAT SHE
had said she would do about Mrs. Post. Of course,
Jessica had never really believed that Joy would tell
Mrs. Post to stop sticking her nose into their business.
But then, she had never expected Joy to do what she
actually did do, either. Jessica really hadn't expected
Joy to do almost exactly the opposite of what she had
promised.

The worst part of it was that Joy had obviously
been planning it for weeks without mentioning it to
Jessica. It all came out on a Friday morning, just a
week before Christmas vacation. Of course Joy tried
to pretend that she was only asking Jessica if it would
be all right, but it was obvious that it was already
arranged—definitely and carefully arranged.

It was not quite time for Joy to leave for work that morning when she came into the living room where Jessica was reading the morning paper.

"By the way, Baby," Joy began, as if what she was about to say were hardly important enough to mention. "I'm thinking of going away on a little trip this weekend—that is, if it's all right with you." She perched on the arm of Jessica's chair and smiled down at her with phony cheerfulness. Jessica sat very still, gripping the arms of the chair and pushing herself back, forcing herself to wait until she'd heard the rest and knew just how much there was to be angry about.

Joy chattered on about how Alan had asked her to spend the weekend at his parents' home in the northern part of the state. But, since Alan's parents were very old-fashioned people who did not approve of divorce, both Alan and Joy thought it would be best if they were given a chance to know Joy a little before they found out that she had been married and had a great-big, almost grown-up daughter. Once they got to know Joy and like her, it wouldn't matter anymore. Then Jessica could go with them to visit, and Jessica would love that because Alan's parents lived on a big ranch where there were all kinds of wonderful things to do. But this time, just this one time, Jessica was to stay home and spend Saturday and Sunday nights in the Posts' apartment. Joy had already talked to Mrs. Post, and it was all arranged.

When Joy finally finished talking, Jessica just went on sitting stiffly, pushing back hard against the chair.

"And I'll be back in time for dinner on Monday," Joy said, "with a nice big present for Jessie." She leaned forward, trying to catch Jessica's eyes. "You do understand, don't you, Baby?" she asked.

"Sure, I understand," Jessica said. "But what if it takes them a long time to get to like you well enough —like five years, or something? Do I get sent to the Posts' for five years?" She jumped out of the chair, almost pushing Joy onto the floor, and ran into her room, locking the door behind her. Joy knocked on the door and called coaxingly, but when Jessica wouldn't answer, she got mad and yelled through the door about what a nuisance Jessica was.

A while later, Joy came back and shouted that she was going to work and they would talk about it some more later, a lot later because she was going to have to work late to make up for missing work on Monday. "So fix yourself a TV dinner, and I'll be home around ten," Joy yelled.

Just before she left, Joy came back once more and rattled the door. Talking in a sweet coaxing voice, she asked Jessica to do the washing when she came home from school that afternoon.

"I'll need some clean things to take along, and I won't have a minute. Old Post will have the laundry room locked by the time I get home. If you'll just put a couple of loads through for me, I'll add a whole dollar to your allowance next week. All right? Jessie Baby, will you do that for me?"

Jessica waited until Joy had asked several times before she yelled, "All right, I'll do it." Then she waited again until the front door of the apartment closed before she came out of her room to stand at the front window and watch Joy walk down the street.

All day long at school, Jessica thought about the coming weekend. She hadn't done that in over a year. Back when she and Brandon were still friends, she had always been thinking ahead to the next weekend. The kind of things they'd liked to do always needed lots of planning and preparation. Jessica had had to make lists—lists of supplies to be gathered, procedures to be followed, and secrets to be protected. Usually, too, there was a lot of reading to be done.

Nearly all the games that Jessica and Brandon had played together were based on books or stories. Plays, Brandon had called them, but they were really just crazy make-believe games. Still she had gone along with all of Brandon's ideas, no matter how crazy, except when they'd had a fight about something and she was really mad.

There had been quite a few fights, of course, but most of them hadn't been her fault. Jessica could remember most of them very well. Like the time during the *Treasure Island* "play" when they had fought over who got to be Long John Silver. It had always been Jessica's part, and it had the best costume. Then one day Brandon decided, for no reason, that he wanted a turn. He had hit Jessica in the eye just because she had kicked him very slightly with her make-believe wooden leg. That time, Jessica had almost had a black eye. Another time, Brandon had very nearly broken her jaw.

That had been during the play about the Black Forest. It had come from a story they had read in one of Mrs. Fortune's old books. Some children had been kidnapped by gypsies and taken into the Black Forest. The children had escaped, but on the way out of the forest, they were chased by a wolf pack. Jessica couldn't remember how many weekends had been spent in the park acting out escapes, wolf attacks, blizzards, and gypsy pursuers. The park gardeners and policemen played the part of the gypsies—without knowing it, of course—but if even one of them saw Jessica or Brandon as they crept across the park, they were captured and had to go back and start over.

The Black Forest play had been one of the best—except, of course, for the day of the fight. That had happened near the tennis courts where they had discovered a bad-tempered German shepherd tied to a bench. Just by accident, Jessica had discovered that the dog could be induced to play the role of a ferocious wolf by simply shaking a big stick over its head. She was acting out the part of the story where the children held the wolves at bay with flaming brands, and it was going very well. So when Brandon yelled at her to stop, she just ignored him. She was jumping in and out and yelling, "Take that! And that," when suddenly Brandon grabbed her by the arm, whirled her around, and socked her hard on the chin.

Afterward Brandon had said he did it because she was hurting the dog, but Jessica had known better than that. She knew he'd done it because she'd thought of such a great way to do the scene, and he was jealous. "You're jealous. You're just a stinking jealous bully! And you broke my jaw. It's broken!"

But Brandon had only grinned maddeningly. "It's not broken." He said. "You couldn't yell that much with a broken jaw."

Jessica had gone home mad, but the next weekend the game had gone on as if nothing had happened.

But those weekends were over now, and the coming one gave Jessica some very different things to think about. There were the long evenings she would have to spend in the Posts' apartment, listening to the constant drone of Mrs. Post's voice and Mr. Post's sports programs on TV. And even worse, there were the days—days that she would have to spend at home alone—except for Worm.

Alone—except for Worm. For three whole days. The thought returned again and again, and with it came a strange calmness. It was as if whatever was going to happen had already happened and there was no longer anything that could be done about it. Her hot frantic anger was gone, too, even when she remembered how sneaky and phony Joy had been. But now and then, beneath the outer numbness, something stirred, like a living pain waiting for the anesthetic to wear away.

When Jessica got home that afternoon, Worm was nowhere in sight. She did not actually look for him, at first, but as she put away her things and gathered up the laundry, she found herself moving cautiously and watchfully, as if the apartment contained an escaped rattlesnake. It wasn't until she had taken the first load of clothing down to the laundry room and returned for the second that she decided she'd better find him. It would be better to find him on purpose than to have him appear suddenly when she wasn't expecting it.

"Besides," she told herself, "if he's asleep somewhere, he's probably in a closet or cupboard where I can shut him in. And then I won't have to worry about him for a while."

It wasn't until she had looked in all his usual hiding places that she noticed that the door to Joy's room was not entirely closed. And that was where she found him—curled up at the foot of the bed, on top of a new red dress.

The dress, still in its fancy striped box, lay on Joy's bed near her partly packed suitcase. The lid was pushed to one side, and Worm had curled up to sleep inside the box, in a nest of tissue paper and soft red material.

"Get off there," Jessica said, grabbing Worm and

throwing him toward the head of the bed. She pushed back the tissue paper and lifted out the dress. It was a beautiful dress, made of a soft wool and trimmed at the hem and around the wide cuffs with bands of real fur.

At first—just for a moment—the dress made her feel good, thinking how great Joy would look in it. She'd really knock them out—those stuffy parents of Alan's and all their dumb friends. But then, as Jessica turned to the mirror, holding the dress up in front of her, her mood began to change.

The red dress reminded her of a picture she'd seen somewhere of a Christmas scene: lots of elegant gorgeous people in a beautiful firelit room, with open snowy countryside showing beyond the frosty windows. That was the kind of place the dress belonged, a place that she, Jessica, would probably never see. A place where no one was even supposed to know that she existed. Wadding up the soft red wool, she threw it on the bed and pounded it with her fists.

Worm was watching—sitting, cool and collected, on a pillow at the head of the bed. As Jessica stopped pounding and started staring at him through hot flooded eyes, his whiskers twitched mockingly. Then, very deliberately and with studied unconcern, he began to wash a front paw. Snatching up the wadded dress, Jessica threw it at him with all her might.

Worm spat and leaped aside, and as Jessica darted after the dress, her face came close to his. Close to—his devil's face, horned and evil, with burning brassy eyes.

There was no time. Not even time enough to try to stop it. The fierce excitement flared, and Jessica collapsed and sat on the edge of the bed, hugging the trembling that had begun deep inside. "What should I do?" she asked soundlessly, and then she waited—quiet, except for the shaking and the thunder of her heart.

The voice came in a low and distant moan. "The labels," it said. "Look at the labels."

Jessica picked up the red dress and read all the labels. The one on the sleeve said, "Size 9" and "$79.95," but at the neck there was another larger label that said, "Rondel Original" and "Dry Clean Only". She turned the dress over, looking for more labels. On the front, near the fur collar, there was a patch of gray cat hairs. She had begun to brush at the hairs with her hand, when the voice came again.

"There are hairs on the dress," it howled. "The dress is dirty."

"Yes," Jessica said, "it's dirty. Maybe it should be——"

"Wash it," the voice yowled. "Wash the dress."

Jessica nodded. She looked again at the label at the neck of the dress. Then she stood up slowly and went into the bathroom to gather up the second load of washing. Wrapping the red dress carefully into the middle of the bundle, she went down again to the laundry room.

When the red dress came out of the drier, it was a shrunken matted rag, trimmed with shriveled strips of stringy fur. Jessica dumped it on Joy's bed with the rest of the wash and went back to her own room. Closing the door firmly behind her, she lay down across the bed.

Lying stiff and straight, staring up at the ceiling, Jessica concentrated on trying to bring back the excitement, the wild and burning joy, but it was gone. Even the anger, like the red dress itself, had shrunk and faded almost beyond recognition. Nothing was left but a strange numbing cold and a feeling of desolation and ruin—a feeling like the ruins of a burnt-out house after a cold wintry rain.

Time passed slowly. Dinner time came and went, and Jessica went on lying across the bed, until at last the numbness deepened and she drifted into restless sleep.

# Chapter Nine

Darkness and a dim uneasy dream disappeared in a blaze of light and sound. Jessica awoke to a blinding light and a loud angry voice. Joy was standing over her, shaking the remains of the red dress and shouting.

Half awake and startled, Jessica put her hands up in front of her eyes—and instantly remembered the ruse that had worked before. She sat up slowly and stared at Joy, letting her eyes go blank and unfocused, and her tongue slur and stumble.

"What is it?" she said. "What happened? I can't remember what happened."

But Joy was not as easily impressed as Mrs. Post had been. "My dress," she stormed. "You ruined my new dress."

"Dress?" Jessica mumbled. "What dress?"

"This dress," Joy yelled. "My new dress. Eighty dollars. Eighty dollars thrown away. The only decent thing I had for the trip."

"Trip? What trip?" Jessica crumpled her face into a tearless lament and began to sob. "My head hurts. I can't remember."

"What do you mean—you can't remember?" Joy had finally begun to notice. She stopped screeching and looked at Jessica with concern. Jessica held her head between her hands and rocked herself back and forth, moaning softly. She had seen a similar part acted in just that way on television. She did it well, and it had the right effect. Joy sat down on the bed and took Jessica's hands and held them in hers.

"Jessica," she said. "What do you mean you can't remember? Tell me about it—and try to make some sense." Joy's voice was still harsh and angry, but her eyes were changing; the burning glare was clouding over with worry and confusion. "Jessie," she said, "what's wrong with you? What is it?"

When Jessica awoke the next morning, Joy was talking on the hall telephone. At first only an occasional word was audible, but her voice got louder suddenly, as if she were arguing.

"Yes, I know," she was saying. "I know, Alan, and I'm terribly sorry. You'll just have to tell them that there was an illness in my family. I simply can't go

away and leave her like this. I don't know. I'm sure it's nothing serious. But I agree that she should have some professional attention."

There was a long pause, and then Joy went on, "Yes, I know there must be, but I can't imagine what it could be. She has been spending more time at home lately, but she seemed happy—I mean, she has her cat and her books. I really think it must be some school problem. No, she hasn't said much about it, but her grades have been worse lately, and she doesn't talk much about her classes. You know how bad city schools are nowadays. If I'd only been able to send her to a good private school, I'm sure this ·wouldn't have happened."

Joy's voice dropped then, but she went on talking for a long time; even when Jessica listened from right behind the door, she could only make out occasional words and phrases. She heard once "terribly expensive," and then something about "special schools for children with that kind of problem." The only other phrase that Jessica caught was an almost whispered, "only as a last resort." By then she was leaning against the door with her ear to the crack, until the door moved suddenly with a creaking noise. Joy stopped talking, and Jessica raced on tiptoe back to bed. A moment later, Joy looked in at her and asked how she was feeling, and when she went back out, she closed the door tightly.

"Only as a last resort." The phrase repeated itself

ominously in Jessica's mind. What was it they were planning—as a last resort? She thought perhaps she knew. Perhaps the last resort would be to send her away to school—perhaps to a school for crazy people, with barred windows and high fences and locked doors. That was something she hadn't counted on. That would be the worst punishment of all, and it wasn't fair. It wasn't fair because it wasn't her fault. None of it had been her fault.

"They can't," Jessica told herself. "They couldn't send me to a place like that, because there's nothing wrong with me. I was just pretending, to make them forget about being angry."

She had only wanted to make them wonder, to give them something to think about. And she had done too good a job. She had pretended too well. She'd always been very good at pretending. Brandon had always said so, and it was because of him that she'd had so much practice at it. If she were sent away and locked up somewhere, it would be his fault. Brandon's fault, and of course, Worm's.

There was only one thing to do. She must get up, get dressed, and go out and let Joy see that there was nothing wrong with her. She'd say she'd been sick and feverish yesterday, but now she was better. She'd heard that people could get funny in the head, delirious, when they had a fever. She'd just say she must have been delirious yesterday, but that now she was herself again. She jumped out of bed and ran to the closet for her clothing.

As she gathered up her clothes, she whispered to herself, "I'll show them. I'll show them there's nothing wrong with me." She was still whispering when she noticed the eyes. There, in the darkest corner of the closet, two eyes looked up at her—Worm's eyes, diamonds lit by cold golden fire.

"Get out," she whispered, kicking in the direction of the eyes. "Get out of there. Get away from me."

But the eyes did not move. Turning on the closet light, she pushed aside the hanging clothing, and there he was—in the midst of a messy nest of shoes and sweaters. He glared up at her, flat-eared and quivering, his face an angry evil threat. With no warning, with not even the familiar rush of sharp excitement, the voice was there.

"There is nothing wrong with you." The words throbbed through her head like the beat of an enormous drum.

"Go away," Jessica whispered. "Go away. I don't want to talk to you. I don't have to talk to you."

"No," the voice said. "You don't have to talk to me. But you have to listen."

"Why? Why do I have to listen? Who sent you?" There was no answer.

"Whoever sent you, she can't make me listen," Jessica said. "I won't listen anymore."

"Nooo," the voice howled. "It is too late." The sound of the voice drifted, swelling and fading, but the meaning was clear. "Too late," it said. "You must listen. When the time comes, you will hear."

Jessica grabbed her clothes and ran out of the room.

Time passed, and the weekend crept slowly by. Worm had said that the time would come; and with a cold unyielding certainty, Jessica knew that what he said was true. But hours passed, and then a day, and the voice was silent. Jessica was very careful. She was careful to stay away from Worm, and careful to act extremely normal and happy when she was around Joy; and she was around Joy almost all weekend. Alan had gone alone to see his parents, and Joy had stayed at home with Jessica. It was the most time they had spent together for almost as long as Jessica could remember. It should have been wonderful. Joy played cards with Jessica on Saturday night; on Sunday, Joy helped her comb her hair in a different style and took her to a movie matinee. But it wasn't right.

None of it was right. Nothing more was said about the red dress—nothing at all. Once when Jessica had lost ten dollars on the way to the grocery store, Joy had raved for a week. But now, with eighty dollars wasted, she acted as if nothing had happened. She was only pretending. Jessica knew Joy was pretending about the red dress and about everything else—trying to act as if she weren't following Jessica's every move, memorizing everything she said. As the hours went by, Jessica felt herself getting more and more nervous and irritable; it became harder and harder to act cheerful and normal. By Sunday evening, Joy's suspicious spying had made her so jumpy that she found herself wishing something she had never wished before—that Joy would go out and leave her alone.

She was actually almost glad when Joy finally said, "I think I'll just drop over to see Betty Moore for a few minutes. You remember Betty, don't you? She had the desk next to mine at the office until last summer. Her baby was born in October, and I've been promising for weeks to get over to see him. You don't mind do you, Baby? This is your favorite TV night, so I know you won't be bored."

Because she was working so hard at acting cheerful, Jessica said, "Sure, go ahead," before it occurred to her that her normal reaction would have been quite different. Normally she would have shrugged resentfully and maybe said that it had been years since she been interested in the Sunday evening kiddie shows— a fact that Joy might have noticed if she ever stayed at home.

Joy was into her coat and out the door very quickly. She was gone before Jessica had time to remember one very important reason why she should have stayed at home. The reason was Worm. With Joy at home, he had been out of sight all weekend; but now she was gone, and Worm would be coming out.

Jessica sat very still and listened. It was quiet in the apartment. Too quiet. Carefully she got up from the couch and started toward her room, but in the hallway she stopped. The door to her room had been left open. He might be in there, under the bed or in the closet. She turned and ran back across the living room and out the front door into the hall.

She was outside the door before she stopped to think about where she was going. There was the secret cave, but it was a very cold night and her coat was in the closet in her bedroom. She would have to stay in the apartment house, and the only person she could, or would, visit was Mrs. Fortune. She had already decided on a visit to Mrs. Fortune, when suddenly she remembered the first words she had heard Worm say. On that first day Worm had said, "Mrs. Fortune knows more than she tells."

Mrs. Fortune would know. Jessica had felt that all along. And suddenly she was no longer afraid to find out exactly how much Mrs. Fortune knew—how much she knew about demons and possession and witches—and about Worm.

When the door opened, Mrs. Fortune, as always, seemed overjoyed. "Well, well," she said. "This is a pleasant surprise. Isn't this is a pleasant surprise, Lucasta?" she repeated to one of the fat white cats who had followed her to the door. Lucasta sniffed at Jessica and backed away, dipping her ears and wincing as if she didn't find Jessica's presence pleasant at all.

Jessica laughed nervously. "I don't think she agrees with you," she said. "She never did like me much."

"Nonsense, my dear." Mrs. Fortune moved with maddening slowness as she led the way to the kitchen. "I think it's just that she smells Worm on you. They always react badly to the smell of a strange cat."

Jessica had planned to lead up to the subject gradually, but Mrs. Fortune had given her such a perfect opening she plunged ahead.

"That's why I came," she said. "I mean that's one of the things I came to talk to you about," she said. "About Worm, I mean. About him being—such a strange cat."

Mrs. Fortune was putting some milk on to heat for cocoa and getting out the jar of molasses cookies. She put the jar in front of Jessica and lowered herself carefully into the chair at the other end of the table. For at least a minute she only smoothed the tablecloth with her warped old hands and nodded musingly. It was impossible to tell if she were nodding in agreement or only from old age. At last she said, "Yes, he is a strange one, my dear." She looked up from the tablecloth, smiling. "I think I mentioned that he looks as if he might be related to a very ancient——"

"I remember," Jessica interrupted. "You said he might be an Abyssinian, or something like that. But that's not what I mean. I'm not just talking about the way he looks. What I mean is—well, do you remember that you said once you thought he'd lived before? That you thought cats really do have nine lives."

"Ah, yes, at least—at least nine," Mrs. Fortune said.

She bent over to pick up Lucasta—or one of the others—Jessica could never tell the fat white cats apart. She put the cat in her lap and crooned over it, seeming almost to forget, for a moment, that Jessica was there.

"Mrs. Fortune." Jessica used the tone of voice teachers used on her when she daydreamed in class. She waited until the cloudy blue cleared from the old woman's faded eyes, and then she went on, "Mrs. Fortune. What do you think about witches? I mean—do you think there is such a thing? Or at least that there might have been once?"

Jessica watched Mrs. Fortune carefully, looking for what might lie behind the wrinkled smile and the dream-dimmed eyes. "I guess not many people believe in such things nowadays," she continued. "But do *you* think there could have been—in the olden days?"

Mrs. Fortune lifted her head sharply. "Ahh," she said. "The milk." She got shakily to her feet, went to the stove, and began to prepare the cocoa. As she moved about, she made sharp little noises to herself from time to time—a kind of ancient coughing or chuckling sound. When she came back to the table with two cups of hot cocoa, Jessica thought she had probably forgotten what they'd been talking about.

But after Mrs. Fortune had lifted the cat out of the chair and sat down with it in her lap, she finally said, "Witches—about believing in witches—it's not a question I'd care to answer for just anyone who

115

might ask. But I can see you have reason for wanting to know. So, I'll tell you this. Belief in mysteries—all manner of mysteries—is the only lasting luxury in life." She stopped for a while and nodded as if agreeing with what she had just said. Then she went on, "Yes, my dear. I'm quite prepared to say that I believe in witches." Her face crinkled into the cozy expression she used when she talked to her white cats. "I believe in the witches of yesterday and today—and in all shapes and sizes."

Jessica pulled her hand away from where Mrs. Fortune's wrinkled claw of a hand had reached out to pat it. She was beginning to feel as if she were being talked down to—made fun of, perhaps, in a very subtle way. She didn't intend to be teased or laughed at like a kid who'd been reading too many fairy stories.

She let her eyes go narrow and leaned forward sharply. "And what about possession?" she asked. "Do you think witches can send their demons to possess other people and make them do what they want them to?"

She had intended to shock—to make Mrs. Fortune take her questions more seriously—but the effect was greater than she had counted on. The old woman sat suddenly more erect; her smile disappeared, and her eyes grew steady and searching. She sat silent, moment after moment, until at last Jessica went on herself.

"There are books that tell about it," she said. "About how demons can be sent in the shape of people or animals to torment people and make them do things. Do you think that can really happen? What do you think, Mrs. Fortune?"

At last, Mrs. Fortune nodded slowly. "Many books and many religions have taught about possession," she said. "Many people have believed in it."

"I know," Jessica said. "I've read about that, too. I just wanted to know about you. I mean—I wanted to know what you thought about it."

Mrs. Fortune flinched suddenly and then chuckled, leaning over to look down at her feet. "Bad boy, Simeon," she said. She leaned farther and gently shoved another of the white cats away from her ankle. "He's jealous because Lucasta has been on my lap for so long. He's always been quite wicked about using his claws to get his way. He's the youngest of my little family, and I'm afraid he's a bit spoiled. He's Sabrina's last kitten you know. The only one in her last litter, and he has always been a pampered baby."

She pulled the huge white monster of a cat up onto her lap beside Lucasta and, almost hidden by cats, she began to pet and talk to them in a voice as private and inward as a purr. She seemed to completely forget about Jessica for several minutes. When she did remember, she struggled to her feet, depositing both cats on her chair.

"But, my dear," she said, "you've finished your cocoa, and there's lots more here waiting for you. You must have another cup."

She poured the cocoa into Jessica's cup and then fussed around the kitchen, wiping up crumbs and putting out fresh water for the cats. Coming back to the table, she pointed under Jessica's chair and said, "Look, my dear."

Jessica looked and picked up an old hand-carved wooden top. It was one of the toys from the Treasure Chest.

"Simeon fished it out of the box the other day and has been chasing it around the floor. Behaving almost as if he were a kitten again," Mrs. Fortune said. Reaching for the top, she cradled it in her two hands and inspected it carefully.

"Just as it was," she murmured. "Just as it was the day old Grindstone carved it for me from the root of the oak tree."

Jessica knew the story. When she and Brandon were small, it was one of their favorites. It concerned a strange old recluse who had lived on the side of a hill near the village where Mrs. Fortune had lived as a child. He had carved her the top after she had helped him put out a fire in his tiny cabin. He had told her that the top was made of magic wood and that it would bring her three adventures. The story of the adventures was very exciting and took a long time to tell. Jessica tried to say that she had heard the story, but it was too late. Once Mrs. Fortune was into a story, there was no use trying to change the subject.

The story went on and on, with more twists and

turnings and long drawn-out suspense than Jessica remembered. She could not keep herself from being halfway caught up in the story; yet she did wonder if someone so old and childish—crazy maybe—could be tricky enough to use a long story to stall for time. It didn't really seem possible but perhaps it was because before the story was finished there was a loud knock on the door.

It was Joy. She had not stayed very long at her friends house and, on arriving home, had not been able to find Jessica. She had tried the Doyles' apartment and the Posts' and then had come to Mrs. Fortune's. She was obviously upset, and she hurried Jessica off, barely giving her time to say good-by.

All the way upstairs, Joy fussed and scolded about the scare Jessica had given her. She didn't seem to remember that Jessica had often been away before when Joy came home, without causing anyone any concern at all. Jessica didn't say so, however, because it didn't need saying. They both knew it was only the other strange things that Jessica had done that made Joy afraid of what she might do next. They were almost to the door of their apartment when Joy suddenly interrupted her lecture to ask, "What? What did you say?"

"Say?" Jessica said. "When? I didn't say anything."

"Yes, you did. I heard you. Something about Mrs. Fortune."

"Oh, yes," Jessica said. "I just said that Mrs. For-

119

tune has been asking me to come and visit her for a long time. But I'm sorry I didn't think to leave you a note."

Actually, the only thing Jessica had said was something she hadn't intended to say out loud at all. Halfway up the stairs, in the middle of Joy's talk on thoughtfulness and responsibility, she had found herself repeating, "Mrs. Fortune knows more than she tells."

# Chapter Ten

On Tuesday morning when Jessica came into the kitchen, she found Joy not only up, but with her hair combed, her eyelashes curled, and all dressed for work. Obviously she'd been up for a long time. And she actually sat down with Jessica to drink her coffee and orange juice.

She was unusually chatty, too. As Jessica ate, Joy jabbered away about nothing in particular for quite a while then finally, with elaborate casualness, she mentioned that she'd made an appointment for Jessica to talk to the school psychologist—only Joy called him the counselor.

"Oh, by the way," she said. "You may be excused from one of your classes today to have a talk with the school counselor. I just thought you——"

"Counselor?" Jessica interrupted. "I never heard of any counselor. What's his name?"

"Weaver, I think. Yes, that's it. Mr. Weaver."

Jessica nodded, narrow-eyed, firming her face against the pang of fear that shivered beneath the surface. "Oh, him," she said. "I've heard of him. Everybody calls him the shrink. That means he's a psychiatrist, doesn't it?"

"No," Joy said quickly. "Not a psychiatrist. He probably has a degree in psychology, but I'm sure that, in a junior high school, he would just be called a counselor. Anyway, as I started to say, I just thought it might be helpful for you to talk over some things with someone outside the family. Not that I think you have any serious problems, because I don't. At least not any more than are normal for a girl your age. But we all need someone to tell our troubles to sometimes. I've thought, lots of times, about going to a psychiatrist myself. And I would have, too, if it weren't so expensive. Lots of my friends are doing it. Half the people Alan and I know go around talking about what 'my psychiatrist' says about this or that. It's quite the *in* thing to do." Joy stopped to catch her breath and smile a bright unreal smile. "You'll be right in style, Baby," she said.

Jessica shrugged, dropping her eyes in case the fear might be showing through. "Okay," she said. "Okay, I'll talk to him."

Joy left then, for work, and Jessica went on sitting

at the table, staring at a spatter of light the crystal sugar bowl made from the sunshine that slanted through the window. But she wasn't thinking about sunshine. Instead she was thinking about the fear and where it had come from, and why? She knew it wasn't Mr. Weaver she was afraid of. She'd never been afraid of anybody like that. In fact, she'd never really been afraid of anything much—except the dream. And now, sometimes, of Worm.

Suddenly she jumped up, slamming her napkin down and almost knocking the chair over backwards. The fear was gone now, burned away in a blaze of anger. "He'd better not tell them to send me away," she said out loud. "He'd just better not."

All the way to school, Jessica thought about the coming interview with Mr. Weaver. She wondered what it would be like. She felt fairly certain that she knew what to expect because she'd done such a lot of reading on the subject. All of Joy's magazines were full of things about psychology. Jessica had read columns by marriage counselors and child psychologists, articles on family therapy, and dozens of surveys on everything from sex to thumb-sucking. She felt fairly certain that nothing that Mr. Weaver might ask her could come as too much of a surprise.

By the time Jessica got to school, she was feeling much better; but the fear came back again briefly when, during second period, she was told to report to the office. As soon as she met Mr. Weaver, however, she began to feel more confident. Mr. Weaver was quite a young man with a warm nervous smile. When Jessica came into his office, he jumped up and held out his hand. "Well, Jessica," he said, "I'm glad to meet you. My name is Roy Weaver. I'm glad we're going to have a little chat today."

"Yes," Jessica said, "I'm glad, too." She sat down in the chair Mr. Weaver indicated, made her eyes wide and friendly, and waited.

She waited for quite a long time. For several minutes she only had to nod and smile as Mr. Weaver made conversation about the school carnival, about how near it was to Christmas vacation, and other topics of general interest.

"Well," he said finally, "as I'm sure you know, your mother has been a bit concerned about you. She feels that something may be worrying you—your classes, perhaps, or a teacher, or even a classmate. I wonder if you feel the same way. Do you think you've been worrying about school lately?"

Jessica nodded slowly. "I guess I have been worrying lately, but not about school. I've been worrying about some things I did at home."

"Umm," Mr. Weaver said. "You mean forgetting about things that happened and——"

"No," Jessica said. She hung her head, looking down at her fingers twisting nervously in her lap. "I guess I didn't really forget. At least not as much as they thought I did. It was just——" She raised her head, catching her breath and letting her chin quiver a little. "It's just that my mother gets so terribly angry when I make a mistake like spoiling her new dress or not doing my work right. I didn't mean to spoil her dress. It was just there, with all her other clothes that she'd told me to wash, and I didn't know it would hurt it. But then when she was so angry, I was frightened——" She let her voice trail away and sat still with her head down.

"And the other time," Mr. Weaver prompted in a very quiet voice.

"You mean the other time I—forgot? Did she tell you about that, too?"

"Well, yes, she did mention it. She said she wasn't there herself, but a friend told her about it."

Jessica sighed. "Mr. Weaver," she said. "I guess you know about how some people have extra good imaginations?"

"I certainly do," Mr. Weaver said. "As a matter of fact, I used to be that kind of a kid myself."

"Me, too," Jessica said. "And sometimes I imagine something so plain that—you know—I almost really think it's there for a minute. Like that man in the back yard. See, Mrs. Post, she's our landlady, is always telling me about murderers and how they're everywhere these days, and how you have to be careful all the time, and I guess she just got me to thinking about them so hard that I thought I saw one. Then when she said she was going to tell my mother

that I told a lie, I was so scared I guess I started acting a little funny."

"I see," Mr. Weaver said. He sounded impressed
and sympathetic, as if he could see how it wasn't
Jessica's fault at all. She let her eyes slide up from
where they were watching her fingers twining nervously
in her lap. He looked impressed, too. "I see," he said
again, and then, "Jessica, I noticed on your records
that you seem to do your best work in English classes.
Is English your favorite subject?"

Jessica looked thoughtful—as if she were trying to
decide very carefully about favorite classes. Actually
she was trying to decide what Mr. Weaver had in
mind now—what he was leading up to. Obviously he
wasn't just asking out of general curiosity; the question
about English must be setting things up for something else. She wondered if there was a particular
subject that was usually picked by people who had to
be sent away to a special school.

"I like reading," she said cautiously. "I read a lot."

"I see," Mr. Weaver said. "How about writing?
Most people who enjoy reading are pretty good writers.
I'll bet you write pretty good stories." Before Jessica
had time to decide on an answer, he went on, "I have
a collection of interesting pictures here, and I was
wondering if you'd like to pick one and write a little
story about it. Now, which one do you think is most
interesting?"

Jessica held back a smile. She understood now. She'd

read about things like that in Joy's magazines. Pictures and toys and games and even inkblots were used to trick people into telling about their problems, and that showed the kinds of things that were really wrong with them. Knowing what she did, she felt sure she'd be able to write the kind of story that would keep Mr. Weaver from finding out anything at all.

At first, for just a moment, she considered writing the truth, writing a story that would explain all about Worm: how he was a demon sent by a witch, and how he was to blame for everything that had happened. But she very quickly gave up that idea. In the first place, Mr. Weaver probably wouldn't believe it; and in the second place, there was no suitable picture among those he had given her.

It would be much safer and easier to write a story that had nothing whatever to do with herself and her problems. She would write a completely "made up" story that would have Mr. Weaver so confused he'd spend hours and hours trying to figure out what it was all about.

The "making up" of the story was no problem. She picked out a picture of a lot of people in a city park. There were boys and girls on skates and tricycles, nursemaids and policemen, and an organ-grinder with a monkey. Near the middle of the picture there was a baby lying on the grass on a blanket. Jessica's story began with a policeman coming up and chucking the baby under the chin and then smiling at a woman, who sat nearby under a tree, to let her see that he thought she had a cute baby. Then other people came up to the baby, kids and grown-ups both, and looked at it for a moment before they went away. Finally, one little kid asked the woman under the tree if she didn't think her baby was getting hungry. The woman said it wasn't her baby, and she thought it belonged to the old lady sitting on the bench. Then the organ-grinder came through the park with his monkey, and everyone got up and followed them. No one looked back to notice that the baby was left behind, all alone in the middle of the grass. Time passed, and no one came back for the baby. It began to get dark and cold. It got darker and colder until finally it was night, and the baby went on lying there alone because nobody wanted it, and nobody ever came back to get it.

Jessica hadn't been able to think of a very good way to end the story, so she copied something from a story she'd read once. In the last sentence she told how the leaves from the trees came down on the baby until it was all covered up.

The story had been easy to write, and afterward Jessica felt pretty good about the way it had turned out. She thought she'd written it well, using plenty of big words. Mr. Weaver would see that she was smart and that there was nothing at all wrong with her brains. She felt good, too, that she'd written about something that would really keep Mr. Weaver guessing—something that had nothing to do with anything real at all.

On the way home from school, Jessica thought over the whole interview with Mr. Weaver. The more she thought about it, the more certain she became that it had gone well. She felt quite confident that Mr. Weaver had been favorably impressed and that he was not going to recommend that she be sent away to a special school or anywhere else.

"So that takes care of Mr. Psychiatrist Weaver," she told herself as she reached the front doors of the Regency Apartment House. "That takes care of him" —she jumped up three stairs at a time—"and special schools"—she jumped up three more stairs—"and Joy"—"and Mrs. Post"—"and——" She reached the apartment door, turned the key in the lock, and ran straight into Worm.

Like a dark shadow he slid out from under the coffee table and stopped, facing her.

"No," she said. 'No! Go away." But it was too late. The howl was already there, distant and indistinct at first, but quickly becoming louder and more clear. Jessica covered her ears with her hands, but the sound only deepened and hollowed, as if it were drifting through an endless tunnel.

"You heard," it said. "You were told what to do, and you heard."

"No," Jessica said. "I didn't hear anything. You weren't there. I knew what to do from reading."

There was no answer except a distant wordless moan, and Jessica began to move away, inching sideways across the room. She had almost reached the door when the moan grew and once more sharpened into words.

"Wherever you are, when the time comes, you will hear," it said.

Jessica darted into her bedroom, slammed and locked the door. Throwing herself on the bed, she pulled the pillow over her head to shut out the sound.

# Chapter Eleven

THAT DAY SOMETHING CHANGED. "WHEN THE TIME comes," Worm had said; and Jessica knew for sure that day that the time would come again, and there was nothing she could do about it. She had tried to stay away from Worm and to tell herself that she did not have to listen to the things he said. But now she knew, with a cold and hopeless certainty, that she did have to listen. She knew that sooner or later, when the time came, the voice would speak again, and she would listen. There was no place she could go to escape; it was no longer any use to try.

Christmas vacation began, and there were two long weeks of time. Two weeks with Joy away at work almost every day, and out with Alan several evenings, and no place and no one for Jessica except the empty apartment and Worm. She no longer even tried to stay away from him. With a strange numb feeling of resignation, she watched him and waited. He followed her around the apartment as he had always done; but long empty days passed, and he remained silent.

Then, on the last day of the vacation, Joy insisted on taking Jessica visiting with her. Joy's friends, the Lindleys, had children only a little younger than Jessica, and Joy insisted that Jessica would have a wonderful time if she went along. But Jessica had been to the Lindleys' before; she knew better.

She was right, of course. The boy, a fat sixth-grader named Patrick, ignored her, and his loud, giggly little sister whispered about her with a girl friend from across the street. Sitting on the front porch, Jessica watched the two little girls play hopscotch on the sidewalk, stopping now and then to look at Jessica and whisper and laugh. After a while Jessica realized that she was listening, waiting and listening, for the voice to begin. It was just beginning, the silence hollowing into a distant howl, when Joy and the Lindleys came out the front door.

"We're lucky, Jessie," Joy said. "Margaret has to go downtown anyway, so she's going to give us a ride home. We won't have to wait for the bus. Isn't that lucky?"

Jessica nodded, still watching the giggly faces of the two girls on the sidewalk. They're lucky, she thought. They're the ones who are lucky.

At last the vacation was over, and Jessica returned to school. She had never liked school; but this time she was glad to have it begin, to have it take her away from Worm and the empty apartment. With something to do, the days went much faster; it was already Wednesday afternoon when she met Mrs. Fortune outside the Regency's front door. Pushing her shopping cart ahead of her, Mrs. Fortune was just starting out for the grocery store.

"Jessica," she said. "You're just the person I've been wanting to see."

"Me?" Jessica said. "What did you want to see me about?"

"Well, for several things, actually." Mrs. Fortune stopped suddenly, looking up with her head cocked on one side. She motioned upwards toward the second floor. "Brandon," she said. "And his trumpet." She listened for a while, smiling and nodding her shaky old head in time to the music. "He plays very well, doesn't he? It's Brandon," she said again, as if Jessica might possibly have some doubt.

"I know," Jessica said. She had been aware of the sound when she was still almost a block from the Regency. Then loudly, to bring Mrs. Fortune's mind back to the subject, she said, "Why did you want to see me?"

"See you?" Mrs. Fortune asked, blank-eyed.

"You said you wanted to see me."

"Oh, yes," Mrs. Fortune said. "For several reasons. I've been thinking a great deal since our last conversation, and I feel that there are some things we should discuss. I wonder if you could come to see me again soon."

Jessica looked at Mrs. Fortune sharply. She wished she knew just what Mrs. Fortune had in mind. If Mrs. Fortune had decided to tell more about what she knew, then Jessica would be glad to pay her another visit. But if Mrs. Fortune was going to ask a lot of questions and expect answers, then Jessica wasn't so sure. She had had her fill of deep significant questions trying to masquerade as casual conversation. She had had her fill of questions no matter who was asking them, and somehow she was especially uneasy about the questions that Mrs. Fortune might ask.

She didn't know why that was true, but it was. If Mrs. Fortune was really just a poor half-crazy old lady, why should it matter what you told her? It shouldn't matter at all, except that if you told her something you wanted her to know, she might be just crazy enough to twist it into something else. Into something, perhaps, that you didn't want her to know at all.

Jessica was still trying to find out what kind of a discussion Mrs. Fortune had in mind when someone swished by on a bicycle and skidded to a stop a few feet away. It was Kevin Mackey, one of Brandon's close friends. Still straddling his bicycle, Kevin stood looking upwards. As soon as there was a momentary

135

break in the blare of trumpet noise, he shouted at the window, "Hey, Brandon!"

A moment later the window opened, and Brandon leaned out with his trumpet still in his hand.

"Hey, I got it," Kevin yelled, pointing to the large black case strapped to the rack of his bicycle. "Come down and see it."

"Hey," Brandon yelled back. "Great!" It was the first time Jessica had heard his voice in a long time, and hearing it gave her a strange feeling. There was a sharp searing shock—but no pain, because anger took its place.

"I'll be right there," Brandon shouted, and his head disappeared from the window. The trumpet stayed there on the sill, its gleaming golden bell projecting a little way beyond the ledge. In just a minute, Brandon came barreling out the front door of the apartment house, almost running into Jessica and Mrs. Fortune.

"Look out!" he yelled, skidding and grabbing both of them to keep his balance. "Excuse me." He backed off, grinning. "Hey, look who I ran into." He turned away. "Hi, Kevin. Let's see it. Is it the one you wanted?" The two of them bent over the case, entirely engrossed in the new horn.

Mrs. Fortune smiled foolishly at Brandon for a long time before she turned back to Jessica and put out her shaky old hand. "So," she said, "you will come again soon—to talk?"

Looking down at the ugly bird-claw hand, Jessica jerked her arm away. "No!" she said, "I don't think I can. I don't have much time." She walked slowly until she was inside the apartment house, and then she began to run—down the hall and up the stairs to her own apartment. Inside she dumped her books on the couch and went to the window. Three stories below, Brandon was showing Kevin's trombone to Mrs. Fortune, pretending to play as he demonstrated the gleaming slide.

She loves that, Jessica thought. Her dear little Brandon showing off for her. It's a good thing I left, or she'd have missed it. He'd never have invited her to look while I was there—for fear I might have too. He'd never have risked that.

Jessica was breathing hard with angry excitement. She turned away from the window and said it again, out loud this time to Worm. "He'd never have risked that."

From across the floor, Worm was watching her, as she had known he would be, sitting sleek and slim, wrapped in the curl of his long tail. "He is taking a risk, though," the howl said. "He is taking a risk with his trumpet."

Even from across the room, Jessica could see the light flowing in the moss-gold eyes. Excitement throbbed in her head like pain, making her feel dizzy. She shuddered and shook her head to clear it. She could almost hear the sound of the trumpet, muted by doors and walls but clear and unmistakable, just as she heard it every day after school.

The yowling voice blended with the sound of the trumpet. "It's still there," it said. "On the windowsill."

"But they'd guess I took it," Jessica said.

"You don't have to take it," Worm answered. "It will be Brandon's fault—for leaving it on the windowsill. For leaving his trumpet on the windowsill where even a little wind might push it over."

Jessica nodded slowly. She went once more to the window and checked to be sure that Brandon was still on the sidewalk with Kevin. She knew his parents would still be at work, so his apartment would be empty; and having come out so fast, he would almost surely have left the door unlocked.

The front door of the Doyles' apartment was not only unlocked, it was standing open. From the doorway, Jessica could see the trumpet gleaming on the windowsill. She eased toward the window and peered out over the edge. The two boys were still standing near the bicycle. Brandon was calling to someone, probably Mrs. Fortune, though she was no longer in sight from where Jessica stood. She moved to the side of the window and then, crouching down, she reached out and touched the warm golden metal of the trumpet's mouthpiece. For a moment she hesitated; then her hand moved ever so slightly, and the trumpet slid forward, teetered, and slid again—over the edge.

Jessica waited only long enough to hear the crash before she ran from the room.

Safely back in her own apartment, Jessica locked the door and leaned against it, breathing hard. It had been a new trumpet, much more golden and shiny than the one Brandon had begun on over a year and a half ago.

"It was a brand-new one," she whispered.

She looked around quickly for Worm, but he had disappeared. The voice was still there, though. It moved in Jessica's mind, thick and slurred, like an enormous sluggish purr.

"It wasn't new for long," the voice gloated.

Jessica shivered. "He'll probably be able to get it fixed," she said loudly.

She saw Worm then, sitting on the windowsill, almost hidden behind the drapes.

"It can probably be fixed," she said again loudly, but there was no answer. Worm sat silently, looking away from Jessica out the window.

At last she turned away, and gathering her books from the couch, she took them into her room and shut the door. She pulled her chair near the window, and choosing a book, she sat down to read.

Outside the window, the pale winter sun had given way to swiftly flowing clouds. They came thicker and faster, until the sky was full of them, twisting and turning, shading from thunderous gray to bloody red where the last rays of sun slipped through. Staring out at the tortured surface of the sky, Jessica began to see pictures that grew and faded with the shifting clouds.

Something fell, from high in the cloudy mountains, down, down, until at last it disappeared beyond the horizon. A human form appeared, strong and stocky, holding something at arm's length—a trumpet, perhaps—until it grew and drifted into—a gingerbread man.

The gingerbread men! That had been at least three years ago. There had been two of them, and they had been given to Jessica and Brandon by the lady who ran the bakery on Spencer Street. They had been a part of her Christmas window decoration, and they were over two feet tall and elaborately decorated with frosting and Christmas candy. But one of the gingerbread men had no head. Someone in the bakery had broken it off. If the gingerbread men had been for eating, it wouldn't have mattered much, but they were too big, and much too stale to be used for that purpose. They were only good as decorations or playthings; so the broken head mattered—a lot. Without much of a fight, Brandon had let Jessica keep the perfect one.

He'd been that way about some things. When it came to the best and the biggest and the most, where other people would care fiercely, Brandon often didn't seem to care at all. He'd shrug and give in, time after time, until she'd begin to think he'd give in about anything; and then just when she least expected it, his

temper would explode and—look out! When that happened, Jessica had sometimes given in herself, or else she had run and thrown something from a safe distance. But whichever she had done, no matter whether she had run or fought or thrown things, it was never very long until everything was just the same as before. The next day would come, and it was all as if nothing had happened. That was the way it had been. But it wasn't that way anymore.

Jessica was still sitting in her chair, staring out at the clouds, when the phone rang. She put down her book and went to answer it.

"Jessica, is that you?" The voice sounded unreal, as cracked and creaky as an ancient record. Then Jessica realized who it must be.

"Mrs. Fortune?" she said. "Is that you?"

"Yes. Yes, it is Mrs. Fortune. Could you come down to my apartment for a moment, Jessica. I want to talk to you."

"No," Jessica said abruptly. "I can't. Not right now."

"But this is important. Of the greatest importance."

"What is it?" Jessica asked. "Why can't you tell me on the phone?"

There was a pause, and then the voice returned, even more quavering and scratchy than before. "Jessica," it said, "I know about Brandon's trumpet. I *must* talk to you about it."

# Chapter Twelve

Jessica made no plans as she walked down the stairs to Mrs. Fortune's apartment. She was good at planning, particularly when she was in trouble, but this time her mind refused to work.

"I know about Brandon's trumpet," Mrs. Fortune had said on the phone, but she had refused to say anything more until Jessica came down to her apartment.

"She can't know," Jessica whispered to herself. "How could she know? How could she?"

The door opened quickly to Jessica's knock, and Mrs. Fortune led her to the living-room couch, instead of to the kitchen and hot chocolate. They were both seated for what seemed like a terribly long time before anyone spoke. Jessica searched Mrs. Fortune's face for a hint of what to expect, but she saw only the dim eyes and the constant wrinkled smile. Jessica felt her own face changing from a cold numbness to a hot and painful searing.

At last, Mrs. Fortune spoke. "Jessica," she said, "this is very hard for me, for both of us. But I've thought it over and decided what must be done. I've decided that someone must tell Brandon what happened to his trumpet. It would be best if you would do it."

"Tell Brandon? Tell Brandon what?" Jessica said.

"That you pushed his trumpet out of the window."

Although Jessica had expected them, the words seemed to explode in her head, sending shock waves crashing into an empty hollow below her ribs.

"I was turning back to wave," Mrs. Fortune went on, "when I saw you in the window. Why did you do it, Jessica?"

"Why?" Jessica repeated, and speaking seemed to unlock her frozen and useless mind. She remembered suddenly a way that had worked before. At once, she put her hands up in front of her face, palms outward.

"I can't remember," she said in a slow stumbling voice. "I can't remember what happened. Everything is blurry in my mind."

From behind her hands, Jessica's sliding glance told her that Mrs. Fortune did not seem as startled and upset as the others had been. "It—it happens to me sometimes lately," she went on. "I get these strange spells—when I do strange things, and afterwards I can't remember."

Mrs. Fortune's pale old eyes remained on Jessica steadily, too steadily for a person who had just heard something so strange and horrible. She just went on smiling and nodding as if what Jessica had just told her was a perfectly ordinary thing.

"Then that is what you should tell Brandon, perhaps," she said at last. "That you pushed his trumpet out of the window because a strange spell that——"

"Tell Brandon that!" Jessica almost shouted. She jumped to her feet. "No! I won't tell him that. I won't tell him anything. Why should I have to tell him? I couldn't help what happened. It wasn't my fault."

"My dear child," Mrs. Fortune said, "fault is an empty word. It is a coin with only one side. It is not a reason or an excuse."

"What does that mean?" Jessica's voice was shaking with anger. "That doesn't make any sense. I don't see why anyone has to tell Brandon anything. It won't fix his old trumpet. And besides, it wasn't my fault. It wasn't my fault."

Jessica was at the door when Mrs. Fortune called after her. "Wait! I'll not do anything until you have time to think about it. I won't tell anyone until to-morrow night. I hope you'll decide to tell Brandon yourself."

Jessica slammed the door behind her and ran for the stairs. "I won't tell him," she told herself as she ran. "I won't. I don't want him to know."

Anger climbed with her as she climbed, until suddenly, on the first landing, she slowed almost to a stop. If she went on up now, to her apartment—and Worm—what would happen? Worm was there, waiting for her. Waiting for her to ask what could be done. What could be done to keep Mrs. Fortune from telling on her. What could be done to—to Mrs. Fortune——

Jessica walked more and more slowly as a strange crawling fear began to creep from under the anger and excitement that filled her mind. A fear deeper and more deadly than the nightmare terror of the dream of the empty house. But just then Jessica's feet, trained from long years of habit, stopped by themselves, outside the door of the Doyles' apartment. Stopped in the very spot where they had stopped for years, while Jessica waited for Brandon to come out. Standing there, knowing that Brandon was only a few feet away, Jessica could see exactly what it would be like.

"No," she whispered with fierce determination. "No, I can't." She turned, and climbing quickly and certainly, went on up the stairs to the apartment.

As soon as the door to the apartment closed behind her, she began to look for Worm. She did not call him. Worm never came when he was called. Instead she walked swiftly from room to room, looking in all his favorite lairs and sleeping places.

It was when she was looking on the windowsill, behind the drapes, that she noticed the change in the sky. The clouds were still there—thick bloated shapes of dirty gray—but now they were no longer racing across the sky. Instead they hung heavy and motionless, bank on bank, frozen into weirdly twisted and contorted shapes. The air was still and breathless, as if the whole world was waiting for some enormous inevitable catastrophe. Turning away, Jessica continued her search.

She came on him at last in the kitchen, where she had looked carefully, only moments before. He stood just inside the door, poised and wary, ready to jump away. As Jessica lunged at him, he leaped aside, arched and spitting. She stopped and came back. Cornering him against the stove, she pounced, seized him, and carried him, fighting and clawing, into the living room.

Dropping him in the middle of the floor, she stepped back and watched as he whirled to face her—a menacing demon—flat-eared and evil-eyed.

"All right, witch's cat," she whispered. "The time has come."

# Chapter Thirteen

"THE TIME HAS COME," JESSICA SAID, AND IMMEDI-ately the answer began. The silence deepened, thickening into a distant roar like the sound of an ocean in a seashell. Then the roar grew and sharpened into a howl. But the howl was formless, without words or meaning.

"Tell me what to do," Jessica said. "She can't make me tell. She shouldn't try to make me, and *she* shouldn't tell him herself either, because what happened wasn't my fault. She knows it wasn't my fault." The howl was changing into word sounds, but words without form or meaning.

"She knows it wasn't my fault," Jessica repeated. "She knows about you, too, even if she won't admit it. She's ugly and horrible, with her stinking old cats, and she knows all sorts of things that she has no right to know. She knows everything because she's a witch. She's an ugly old witch, and she knows too much. She sent you here to torment me, and it's all her fault, all of it."

"A witch." At last the voice became words. "She is a witch," it said.

Jessica leaned forward, shuddering with angry joy. "Yes," she said. "Mrs. Fortune is a witch, and we've got to make her leave me alone."

"She must be punished," the voice crooned. "Witches must be punished.

"But how? How can we do it?"

"In the old ways," Worm answered. "In the old days, witches were punished by water or by fire."

"But how?"

"Downstairs," the voice was dwindling so that Jessica strained to hear it. "Downstairs. Water and fire. You will know."

When Jessica left the apartment, she did not know where she was going. At least she didn't think she knew, but something led her without hesitation to the laundry room in the downstairs hall. At the door to the laundry room Jessica stopped and looked back for a moment. Across the narrow hall stood the only door to Mrs. Fortune's apartment.

In the laundry room, piles of dry clothes sat in baskets and on the folding table. There was water, dripping from a leaky faucet, and in the corner, the flame that burned beneath the water heater cast a reddish glow. In the cupboard, where Mr. Post kept his cleaning supplies, were large cans of cleaning solution marked *Caution* and *Highly Inflammable*.

If the cleaning solution spilled and ran out the door and across the hall—and if it happened tomorrow during the noon hour, when nearly everyone in the apartment was away, and when Mrs. Fortune always took a midday nap——

"Well, Jessica."

Terror, striking like lightning, spun Jessica to face the quavering voice. Mrs. Fortune was standing in the doorway of the laundry room.

"Well, Jessica," Mrs. Fortune said again, smiling as always. "I didn't expect to see you again so soon."

"N—no," Jessica managed. "I—didn't—expect—either——"

Mrs. Fortune shuffled around Jessica to the clothes dryer. "I just remembered that I left my towels in the dryer," she said.

She bent slowly and painfully over the dryer and pulled out several towels. She had carefully wrapped them into a bundle before she turned again to Jessica, who still stood stricken into a statue of guilty fear. For a moment she returned Jessica's gaze, a sharp, clear steady look, before it faded into her creased and constant smile.

"Good night, my dear," she said, and shuffled past, but halfway across the hall she stopped. "Oh, yes," she said. "I keep forgetting to tell you. I think I found a book of yours the other day."

"A book?" Jessica said. "What book?"

"The library book—about the Salem trials. It must have been months ago that you asked me if I'd seen it. And then, just the other day, when Mrs. Post came in to help with the cleaning, we came across it. It must have slipped down——"

"Oh, yes," Jessica said. "That was the book I lost the night I found Worm."

"If you'll wait for just a moment——" Mrs. Fortune disappeared into her apartment and returned with a book.

"Here you are," she said, handing the book to Jessica. "I'm afraid the fine must be very high by now."

"I've already paid for the book," Jessica said. "They said I had to pay for it because I couldn't find it."

"Well, now that *is* too bad. Perhaps they'll give you the money back if you return it. You can blame it on an old lady's poor housekeeping. You can say it was my fault——"

Jessica turned and ran; she went blindly and in terror.

Turning into the main hall, she almost ran into Joy. Joy stared at Jessica in amazement.

"Jessica," she said. "What on earth!"

"Hello," Jessica said, trying to shape a smile. "Are—are you just getting home?"

"Well, yes," Joy said. "But what on earth were you doing?"

"Just hurrying," Jessica said. "I'd been—downstairs —and I was hurrying to get home, so you wouldn't worry."

"Well," Joy said. "How nice. How nice that you're suddenly becoming so considerate." Her smile said she was amused at the obviousness of Jessica's lie.

They walked together up the stairs to their apartment while Joy complained about the weather and her aching head.

"I don't understand it," she said. "I never have headaches. It must be this crazy weather. It has everyone nervous and on edge. Those awful clouds—and the air is like the inside of a tomb. I just wish that whatever it's going to do, it would do it and get it over with."

At dinner, Joy announced that she and Alan were going to a movie. She looked carefully at Jessica. "You've been awfully funny tonight," she said. "Like you were a million miles away. Are you sure you're all right?"

"I'm all right," Jessica said. "I'm fine."

"You're sure? I wouldn't go out, but this terrible weather has really got me down and I need something to take my mind off it. I won't go, though, if you need me. Do you have something to do."

"Yes," Jessica said. "I have something to do. I have a book to read."

Once Joy was gone, Jessica went to her room, locked the door, and began to read. She skimmed quickly over the first few chapters, the ones she had read before. She remembered parts of them very well. Especially about Ann, the twelve-year-old girl who had become famous. Further into the book, Jessica read some things she didn't remember quite so well. They seemed familiar only in the way strange places suddenly seem familiar—as if you have seen them before. This part of the book told how Ann had been tormented by demons, demons she said were sent by the witches, and how she had accused the witches in the trials before all the people of the community. Afterward, for a long time, Ann had been pitied and honored and feared by everyone.

Then came a part that Jessica had not read before, a part where the witches were condemned to die—old women and young, a man, and even a little girl.

At last Jessica came to the final chapter. It told about a day in August, many years later, when a pale and sickly Ann, now a young woman, stood up before the people of her community and confessed. The demons who had tormented her in her unhappy childhood, she said, had not been sent by the people who had been accused and executed.

Jessica sat staring at the last page of the book. Her eyes were wide, but they no longer saw the printed words or even the book itself. What they did see made her face crumple as if in pain and her head shake slowly from side to side. Her lips moved, from time to time, in a soundless whisper.

At last she dropped the book and lay down across the bed with her face buried in her arms. She lay without moving for a long time.

# Chapter Fourteen

It was almost ten o'clock when Jessica lifted her head from her arms and looked around. She got up, went into the bathroom, and washed her face in cold water. Then she went out of the apartment and down the stairs.

In the downstairs hall, she went directly to the door of Mrs. Fortune's apartment. Because she knew that Mrs. Fortune might already have gone to bed, she knocked as loudly as she could. But almost immediately she heard, from inside the apartment, the sound of movement. A moment later the door opened. Mrs. Fortune was not ready for bed, and in the strange way she had of knowing things, she seemed to be expecting Jessica's arrival. Leading Jessica into the living room, she made no comment of surprise.

Sitting again on the couch in Mrs. Fortune's living room, Jessica stared down at her hands clutching each other in her lap. Several times she raised her head and tried to begin, but each time she failed.

At last Mrs. Fortune said. "What is it, Jessica? Is there anything I can do to help?"

"Yes," Jessica said in a voice she hardly recognized as her own. "You can help me get rid of Worm. I have to get rid of him."

"Get rid of Worm," Mrs. Fortune said. "Why must you do that?"

"You probably won't believe me," Jessica said in the strange tense voice. "But I guess you would if anybody would. It's because he isn't a cat at all. He's a demon. He talks to me and tells me to do terrible things."

Jessica would not have been surprised if Mrs. Fortune had reacted with horror, disbelief, or even amusement. But there was no sign of any such reaction. Instead the pale old eyes remained steady and intent.

At last she said, "Worm is not a demon, Jessica. He is only a cat. If there is a demon in Worm, it is not of his own making. You must get rid of the demon, but not of Worm himself."

"But how? How can I do that?"

"How?" Mrs. Fortune repeated. "Well, let me think."

She thought for a long time, so long that her old head began to nod and shake, and Jessica thought frantically, Oh no! She isn't going to get forgetful and crazy again. Not now.

But then, just as Jessica was beginning to despair, Mrs. Fortune got to her feet and went to the bookshelf at the other end of the room. She began to take down books, look at them, and put them back. At last she kept one and walked to her chair, holding it. It was a very old book with a scuffed and faded binding, the color of dry earth. Inside the small print had a cramped old-fashioned look.

"There you are," she said. "Page ninety-one. That will tell you exactly how it is done."

There was a title at the top of the page. The capital letters were so ornate that Jessica could barely make out the words *Ceremonie for the Exorcism of Evil Spirits*. Glancing down the page, it seemed to Jessica that the ceremony was very elaborate and complicated.

"Will you do it for me?" she asked. "I could go up and get Worm and bring him down here."

Mrs. Fortune shook her head. "No," she said. "I can't do it for you. This is something you must do by yourself. We all invite our own devils, and we must exorcise our own. Read the instructions carefully and follow them as closely as possible. The ritual is very powerful. Ritual and ceremony have always been one of the greatest sources of power. But one thing is of even greater importance: the inner power of your own mind. If you know your mind—and what it is you want—the ceremony will be successful."

Jessica got back to her own apartment barely in time to get undressed and into bed before Joy returned from her movie. After Joy had gone to bed, Jessica sat up reading the instructions for the exorcism over and over again. She listed all the objects she would need and decided where she could get each one. Then she set herself to memorizing the chants and exhortations.

It was very late when she turned out the lights, and it wasn't until then, lying there in the dark, that she began to think again about Brandon and the trumpet. In the empty silence of the night, the thought grew, twisting and turning through her mind, so that sleep would not come. She tried to think of other things, but nothing worked until, in the midst of tossing and turning, she remembered something that Mrs. Fortune had said. The memory came suddenly and so clearly that Jessica could almost hear the creak and rasp of Mrs. Fortune's voice. "The ritual is very powerful," it said.

"By fire and water I conjure thee——" Jessica began, and before she got even to the end of the verse, she had fallen asleep.

The next morning Jessica awoke late and hurried to school in a sleepy daze. The clouds of the day before still hung heavy in the sky, pressing their strange dark shapes even closer to the earth. And in Jessica's mind

strange shapes brooded, too, just beyond the horizon of consciousness. She sat in classes and stared at teachers, who seemed to move their mouths soundlessly while other words and phrases wove in and out through the heavy air.

"We all invite our own devils—it would be best if you would tell him yourself—the demon is not of Worm's making—a witch must be punished—you must know what it is you want—I won't tell Brandon. I won't—by fire and water I conjure thee."

The day seemed endless. Even the clocks seemed to tick more and more slowly in the thick breathless air. Not only Jessica, but everyone else seemed to be waiting uneasily for something to happen. But the calm held, and the clouds hung silent and heavy, until at last the school day was over. Jessica was on her way home when the first drops of rain began to fall—only a few at first, like great cold tears, leaving fat round blotches on the sidewalk.

Just as she reached the apartment house, the wind arrived in an angry blast, whipping her hair and skirt and almost blinding her with flying dust and debris. Safely inside the hall, she rubbed her smarting eyes and pushed the hair back out of her face. Rain was breaking now in waves on the glass door, and the first dusty roar of wind had become a long wet whine. For several minutes, Jessica stood staring while the storm grew in force and intensity. It was as if the whole world were caught up in a fit of terrible anger—spiraling endlessly to some unthinkable climax. At last she turned away, shivering, and climbed the stairs. At the door of her own apartment, she paused briefly with her hand on the doorknob, then opened the door and went in.

She looked for Worm first, moving cautiously and silently. She found him in one of his favorite places, curled into a ball on the floor of the kitchen broom closet. She barely managed to slam the door in his face as he tried to dash out into the room.

"Stay there," she said, "until I'm ready for you."

She hurried then, gathering the supplies she would need for the ceremony. Most of the things were easily available, but there were some problems—some places where substitutions would have to be made. The book called for a chalice and a thurible, the first filled with water and the second with earth. Judging by the illustrations, Jessica decided that chalices and thuribles were fancy metal bowls, so she substituted a silver candy dish and a steel mixing bowl. The earth was a problem because of the storm, until Jessica remembered the potted geranium on the kitchen windowsill.

When everything was arranged in the middle of the floor, Jessica skimmed over the rules for the ritual one last time. Everything seemed to be ready. She had only to set fire to the lumps of charcoal arranged on the layer of earth in the second bowl and it would be time to bring in Worm. She lit the coals, but even after they were burning well, she went on kneeling in the middle of the floor.

In a moment she would go and get Worm, and the ceremony would begin—but what then? Would the exorcism work? Would Worm become a normal cat, and would the voice be silent? Would the voice be silent even during the ceremony, or would it begin to speak—telling her to——

Blazing, blinding light and then a heart-stopping smash of sound swept doubts and thoughts away. They left Jessica standing against the wall, staring toward the windows where the storm lashed and roared and then convulsed again in shattering light and sound.

I'd better hurry, Jessica thought senselessly, before it's too late. She turned toward the kitchen and the closet where Worm was waiting.

When Jessica opened the door to the closet, Worm pressed himself back against the farthest wall. His eyes, dilated from the darkness, were pools of night ringed with narrow rims of gold. It had been a long time since Jessica had touched him except in anger. Now she hardly dared to try. Finally she shoved one foot forward, and as his eyes shifted to follow it, she bent quickly and grabbed him behind the neck. He screamed and fought, struggling to reach her hands with wicked slashes of his hind claws, as she carried him into the front room and dropped him in the middle of the floor.

But the moment Worm hit the floor, he dashed away, disappearing from sight beneath the couch. Prodding him with a yardstick, Jessica caught him again and carried him to the middle of the floor, only to have him dash for the couch again the moment she turned him loose. After one last try and another escape, she finally hit on a solution. In the coat closet she found an old sweater, and after dragging Worm from under the couch one more time, she wrapped him tightly in the sweater, tying the arms around him like a straight jacket. She placed him then, bound like a mummy, in front of the bowls of earth and fire and water, where he remained, a mummy cat, helpless and motionless. Only his head seemed alive—ears back and quivering, hooded angry eyes darting to watch Jessica's every move.

Opening the old book to page ninety-one, Jessica propped it in front of her as she knelt before the chalice and thurible. It was almost dark in the room now, although it was not yet five o'clock. Outside the windows, the storm moaned and wailed, trying to get in. The glow from the burning coals was deepening, turning Worm's eyes from gold to red.

Jessica sprinkled a handful of salt across the water in the first bowl, and bending low, she breathed the first verse of the incantation across the surface.

"Water and salt—where you are cast—no spell or adverse purpose last."

Worm yowled and spat and twisted against his

bonds, rocking his body from side to side. Jessica took another handful of salt and threw it on the burning coals, where it burned brightly in a spatter of tiny sparks. As if in answer, a bolt of lightning burned across the sky.

Jessica bent over the fire and chanted the second incantation: "Creature of fire—this charge I lay—no phantom in thy presence stay."

Worm struggled again more fiercely than before, and Jessica watched anxiously as, still wrapped and tied, he seemed for a moment to stand almost erect on his hind feet. At last he collapsed again and lay still. He did not move as Jessica sprinkled him with water and earth and repeated the third and last verse of the incantation.

"By fire and water I conjure thee—all powers of adversity—banish hence—so might it be."

Jessica had barely finished saying the last word when the door of the apartment banged open and Joy burst into the room, wet and dripping.

"Surprise, surprise, I'm home early," she said. And then, "What on earth's going——"

Jessica's shout of warning interrupted her, but she did not react in time to close the door before a gray shadow flashed by her ankles and out into the hall. Worm had broken loose from his bindings and was making his escape.

# Chapter Fifteen

As Worm dashed past Joy and out into the hallway, Jessica jumped to her feet with a wail and ran after him. She was halfway down the first flight before Joy recovered enough to start shouting.

"Jessica. Where are you going? Come back here and——"

But by then Jessica was on the second flight, and the thudding of her own feet, blending with a drum roll of thunder, drowned the rest of it completely. Ahead of her she saw Worm reach the ground floor and pause for a moment, looking around. He turned to the right, toward the front hall and street entrance.

Jessica was thinking, Ah, no cat door there. He's trapped himself, when she heard a shout and a heavy metallic clatter. She rounded the corner at the foot of the stairs to see Brandon standing in the open door-way, his bicycle on the floor at his feet. He was trying to hold the door open against a torrent of wind and rain, and at the same time pick up his bicycle and get it into the hall. Jessica dashed to the door, and bracing herself, managed to push it back against the wind enough so that Brandon could untangle himself from his bicycle and pull it inside.

"Was that your cat?" Brandon asked as soon as the closing door shut out the roar of the wind. "I was trying to get my bicycle in, and I saw him coming. I tried to grab him, but all I did was drop my bicycle and fall over it."

"Where did he go?" Jessica asked, opening the door enough to peer out into the blinding rain. "Did you see which way he went?"

Brandon propped his bicycle against the wall and came back to help hold the door open. "No, I didn't see," he said. "After that one grab, I was too busy falling over my bicycle. But he got out the door. I know that much."

They peered out into rain that seemed to break against their faces in waves. A car passed, headlights on and windshield wipers flopping. A moment later, from halfway down the block, there was a squeal of brakes.

"Oh, no," Jessica said and ran, Brandon after her. When they reached the spot, the car was starting up again. The driver, who was just rolling up his window, saw them and rolled it back down.

"Was that your cat?" he yelled. When Jessica nodded, he said, "Well you better catch him quick or he's not going to last long—running out in front of cars like that."

They ran across the street and stopped, not knowing which way to turn, until a woman, struggling with her umbrella in a doorway, pointed to the right. They ran that way.

They were running into the wind, blinded and almost drowning in the driving rain. Suddenly Brandon shouted.

"There," he yelled. "There he is. I saw him for just a second. He must have turned down the alley."

Water rushed like a shallow river on the pavement of the alley, but the high narrow walls offered some protection from the blowing rain. They ran down the alley, checking all possible hiding places, behind boxes and garbage pails and in doorways, finding nothing. Yet when they reached the dead end of the alley, there was no sign of Worm.

"He must have gone over the fence," Brandon said. He ran back for a packing box, put it against the fence, and jumped up on it.

"There he is," he yelled, and disappeared over the top of the fence.

Jessica pushed back strands of soaking hair that a blast of wind had plastered across her eyes and struggled up onto the box. As her face cleared the top of the fence, it was suddenly exposed to the full force of the storm. It pounced like a living thing, beating and shaking her and lashing her face with whips of rain. She crouched back down behind the wall, cowering in sudden terror. She leaned against the fence, pressing her face against its rough wet surface.

"Jes—ss—sic—caa!" The wind played with Brandon's shout, stretching it like a rubber band and snapping it back together again.

Bracing herself and wincing, Jessica jumped to her feet and scrambled over the fence, landing with a thud and a muddy slide that carried her down several feet below street level.

The area on the other side of the fence was the construction site for a new apartment building. Excavation had been made for the basement, and scaffolding was in place around bare metal girders. Jessica skidded to a stop against foundation framing and worked her way along it to the corner.

As she turned the corner, she saw Brandon part way up a scaffolding ladder.

"He's up here," he yelled. "He climbed the scaffolding. I think I can——"

He broke off, leaning around the ladder to look upward at something Jessica couldn't see. He yelled something unintelligible that broke off sharply. After a moment, he began to climb down the ladder. Jessica met him at the bottom.

"He fell," Brandon said. "He was way up near the

top, and he tried to jump from the scaffolding to a girder. His claws slipped on the metal, and he fell. It's a long way, more than three stories. He must be dead."

Brandon hurried off, skidding along the steep slope that ended at the edge of the foundation, until he came to steps leading down into the basement area. But Jessica stayed where she was, stunned by a strange shocking pain. "Worm," she whispered to herself. "Oh, Worm."

She was still standing, statuelike, when she realized that Brandon was scrambling toward her on the slope. He was making very little progress, stumbling clumsily and sliding backward almost as fast as he climbed. Finally he seemed to give up and stop trying. Straightening up, he called to her.

"Come on, Jessica, let's go this way. We'll never get back up to the fence again." When Jessica still stood without moving, he yelled again, "Come on. I have him. I think he's alive." It wasn't until then that Jessica realized that he was carrying something cradled in his arms.

Worm didn't look alive at all—not at first. He lay perfectly still, wet and limp, with hanging head and closed eyes. But as Jessica took him in her arms, he made a gasping sound, and she could feel that he was still warm.

"He'd have been dead for sure," Brandon said, "but the basement is flooded. There's about a foot of water where he hit. It must have broken his fall. I think he's just stunned, and nearly drowned. But I don't think anything's broken. Here, let's see his legs."

As Jessica held Worm, Brandon felt his legs one by one and ran his fingers down his neck and back.

"He feels okay," he said. "Come on. Let's get him home before we all drown."

Brandon remembered a gate in the high board fence on the left side, where there was no slippery hill to climb, and they made their way toward it slowly, slipping and sliding—shaking with cold.

It wasn't until then that Jessica realized that she was very, very cold. She had run out of the Regency without even a coat; the icy rain had long ago soaked through to what seemed to be the very center of her bones. Only one spot of living warmth remained, the place where Worm huddled soft and wet against her chest. Shaking so hard that her back ached and her legs trembled under her, she followed Brandon along the fence and around piles of pipes and lumber, slipping and stumbling in the near darkness. They reached the gate at last, only to find it closed and locked.

They had to go on then all the way to the other side of the block, where there was another gate that Brandon was sure would be open.

"Or at least there'll be someone there to let us out. The watchman's shack is right beside the gate, and there's always someone in it."

Jessica nodded, but by then she was so cold and exhausted she'd given up believing they were ever going to get out. Feeling certain she would never again be safe and dry and warm, she trudged and stumbled and shook the driving rain out of her mouth and eyes. Somewhere between the two gates, she began to cry.

She cried steadily as they made their way down the west side of the block, around piles of building materials and over muddy mounds of earth. She went on crying while they roused the watchman—listened to his shocked and indignant sermon about "the dangers of playing in construction sites, and in such weather"—and continued to cry the remaining three blocks back to the Regency. She cried wildly, steadily, as if to make up for all the years that she had not cried at all. But her hot tears were lost in the cold tears of the storm, and the wind out-howled her loudest sobs. No one knew that she was crying at all, except perhaps Worm, lying limp and quiet in the shelter of her arms.

When they reached the Regency, Brandon suggested they go in the back way and clean up in the laundry room before they got to the front hall with its wall-to-wall carpeting.

"Mrs. Post would really wring our necks," he said, "if we tracked up her precious rugs."

Following him around the building and in through the back door, Jessica managed to still her sobs and stop the flow of her tears. But when they stood facing each other in two widening mud puddles in the middle of the laundry-room floor, she was completely unable to speak.

Brandon wiped the rain out of his eyes and looked at her and down at himself. "Wow," he said ruefully, shaking his head, "talk about drowned rats. How's the cat?"

They both looked at Worm. He was stirring a little, lifting his head and opening his eyes.

"He's coming to," Brandon said. "Here, let me hold him while you clean up." He reached out to take Worm from Jessica's arms.

But Jessica backed away, and the tears began again, burning down her cheeks.

"No," she almost shouted. "No! I smashed your trumpet. I pushed it out the window."

Brandon looked dumfounded. "What are you talking about?" he said. "What's the matter with you?"

Jessica laughed—and cried at the same time. "What's the matter with me? I'm a witch—that's what's the matter with me. Didn't you know?" And she turned and ran down the hall and up the stairs.

# Chapter Sixteen

WHEN JESSICA AWOKE, THE SILENCE THAT COMES TO the city only in the early hours of morning told her the night was almost over. Consciousness came slowly and evenly, a smooth and easy floating upward from the depths of sleep. Fully awake at last, she lay very still.

She knew she was awake because she was aware of the silence and of the warm familiar comfort of her bed. She was also perfectly aware of what had happened. All the events of the night before were clear and ordered in her mind. It all came back without trying to remember and, more strangely, without trying—as she had so often done before—*not* to remember. She had only to lie perfectly still, limp and empty, and let it all happen over again in her mind.

She had still been laughing and crying at the same time, when she got back to the apartment with Worm; and Joy, who was already terribly upset, had immediately become hysterical and sent for a doctor. The doctor hadn't wanted to come out in the storm, but Joy had been so frantic, crying and insisting that Jessica was completely hysterical, that at last he had agreed.

By the time the doctor arrived, Jessica was better, and she was able to tell him fairly calmly about the chase through the storm after Worm and about Worm's accident. After he had examined Jessica, the doctor told Joy that it was mostly a case of exhaustion and exposure, and that anyone would be a little hysterical after being out in such a terrible storm. But Joy had wanted Jessica to have a tranquilizer or a sleeping pill, and at last the doctor had agreed—if Joy would take one, too. Before he left, the doctor examined Worm.

Worm, still very damp, bedraggled, and limp, was lying in a padded box beside Jessica's bed. She knew he was still far from well when he let the doctor prod and poke him without a fight. But the doctor said he could find no sign of serious injury.

"He's probably only very bruised and sore from the fall," the doctor said. "He should be showing signs of recovery soon. If he isn't up and eating by tomorrow, I'd certainly take him to a vet."

The doctor left, and a short time later Jessica had

another visitor. This time it was Brandon. If Joy had asked Jessica whether or not she wanted to see Brandon, she would have said no. But Joy hadn't asked. She had simply come into the room with Brandon and pulled up a chair for him near Jessica's bed.

"Now don't stay too long," she'd told him. "She's had a sleeping pill, and she's very tired." Then Joy went out and left Jessica trapped and helpless. She knew she was never going to be able to speak to Brandon ever again, so she turned her face to the wall and waited for him to leave.

"Hey," Brandon said as soon as Joy had gone. "What a night. I haven't had so much excitement since——" Brandon's voice trailed off, and Jessica could feel him looking at her, but she went on staring at the wall.

After a while, Brandon began again. "You know where I've been for the last hour? I've been down talking to Mrs. Fortune. I was really going crazy with curiosity about the things you said—in the laundry. So I called up, but your mother said the doctor was coming and everything, so then I thought about Mrs. Fortune. You know how she knows just about everything, and something told me she'd know something about whatever it was you were talking about. So I went down, and we've been talking until just now."

Before she could stop herself, Jessica burst out, "What did she say about me? What did she tell you?"

"Well, I told her what you'd said about the trumpet, and she told me a little about that."

Jessica turned her face away again. "I'll pay for it," she said. "I'll save some money and pay for it."

"Well, that's okay," Brandon said. "The guy at the shop said he could fix it. And Dad thinks our insurance will cover it. No problem. The only thing is—why? I mean, why did you do it? Mrs. Fortune said something about your being angry, but she wasn't too clear about it." From the sound of Brandon's voice, Jessica guessed he was smiling—the way he always did about Mrs. Fortune and other things he liked. "She was in one of her more mysterious moods," he said. "I couldn't figure it out exactly. I mean—what were you angry about?"

That was too much. Jessica whirled around and faced Brandon. "What have I got to be angry about? Nothing at all! Just that after we'd been friends for years and years, you found somebody new and you told me to get out." Jessica's voice was shaking, and her skin felt tight and hot across her cheekbones.

Just as he had done in all their fights, except for the rare times when he was the angry one, Brandon only nodded with a maddeningly peaceful smile. "Just like old times," he said, which was so close to what Jessica was thinking that it momentarily destroyed the full force of her anger.

"Okay," Brandon said. "I did tell you to get out, and it was a crummy thing to do. But afterward I tried to tell you about it, and you wouldn't listen. I tried to tell you that I'd just met Kevin and Jay, and I'd been wanting to get to know them, and all the way home that day they'd been talking about football and stuff like that and what a pain girls were. Then we got to the apartment, and there you were waiting in the hall with all those spears and helmets and stuff for—whatever play we were going to do that day——"

"Alexander the Great," Jessica said. "We were doing the second act."

"Yeah," Brandon said. "Anyway, I didn't mean for you to get out for good."

"And that's supposed to make everything just fine," Jessica said. "I'm supposed to be absolutely overjoyed that all you meant was that I was supposed to stay out of sight when your important school friends came around."

"I know. No excuse. Except that you were the one that always said the plays were stupid baby games and that everyone would laugh at us if they knew about them."

"I didn't mean it," Jessica said. "I only said that when I was mad."

"And the next day I tried to talk to you and tell you I was sorry, and you said you weren't ever going to speak to me again."

"I didn't mean that either. Don't you have enough sense to know that people don't mean it when they say things like that?"

"People ought not to say things they don't mean,"

Brandon said.

"But everyone does," Jessica said, "nearly everyone." She turned back toward the wall, and for a long minute there was a strained uncomfortable silence; yet Jessica knew, as she had often known with Brandon, that they were thinking about the same thing. There was something else to be explained.

They both started at once. "Why did you say——" Brandon began just as Jessica started, "About being a witch——" They both stopped and looked at each other for a moment before Jessica looked away. Staring down at the bedspread, she said, "I really think I am one. I must be."

"Why?"

Jessica shook her head. "It's too crazy. It's too—awful."

"Look," Brandon said, "I know quite a bit about witches. I mean, I've done some reading about them."

"It started a long time ago," Jessica said. "With Worm—it started with Worm."

She told Brandon about all of it from the very beginning when she had found Worm in the cave. She left nothing out, not even the smashed trumpet, and the thing she had almost done—the thing that was so terrible it still made her scared and sick even to think about it.

Brandon listened without saying a word, only nodding his head at times, and now and then leaning over to look at Worm where he still lay limp and

motionless in the padded box. When she was finished, he was silent for a long time before he said, "I still don't see why you think you're the witch."

"It must be me," Jessica said. "Last night—it seems like years ago, but it was only last night—after I finished reading the book about the Salem witches, I decided that I must be one. All of a sudden I saw how none of the people who were accused were really guilty. It was just that Ann and the other girls found out how much power they could have by making people believe that nothing they did was their fault. So then I thought that Ann and the others were the real witches—and all of a sudden I knew I was, too. And if Worm was a demon, I must have been the one who made him that."

Brandon leaned over again to look at Worm. "I wonder if it worked. The exorcism, I mean."

Jessica leaned over the box, too. "I don't know. I'd just barely finished, and I don't know if I even did it right. Mrs. Fortune said the most important thing was to be sure of what you wanted to happen, and I *was* sure of that. But I wasn't at all sure about the rest of it."

Brandon reached into the box and put his hand on Worm's side where the steady beat of his heart could be seen under the soft gray fur. He nodded knowingly, like a doctor making a diagnosis. "I think it worked," he said. "At least partly. These things usually take some time."

"Oh yeah?" Jessica said. "What do you know about it?"

"A lot. I told you I'd been doing some reading on the subject of witches and demons and all kinds of stuff like that. I've had a lot of books out of the library."

"So that's where they all were," Jessica said, but Brandon wasn't listening. His eyes were glazed over with concentration, the way they'd always been when he was getting an idea for a play.

"But there's a lot I haven't read. We'll check out everything we can find on the subject, and we'll set up a re-training schedule. A rehabilitation program— for ex-demons."

"How?" Jessica asked skeptically. "How are you going to do it?"

Worm lifted his head, and flattening his ears threateningly, he struggled to get away from Brandon's hand. Brandon took his hand out of the box.

"I'm not sure yet. Not entirely. But I think the first step will be to get him to trust us. That's always the first step. We'll set up a kind of clinic with daily treatments. We'll make a list of them and keep track of the results. You can be in charge of that. Maybe we'll get some other patients, too. My aunt just got this Pomeranian that could probably use a little therapy, too."

Jessica had been very quiet, and at last Brandon stopped planning and looked at her. "Do you want to

181

try it?" he asked.

Jessica nodded. Her throat felt strange, so tight and painful that she didn't dare try to speak.

Just before he went out, Brandon said, "Oh, yeah, there's one more thing—about your being a witch. I don't think you could be. At least not anymore."

"Why not?" Jessica managed to ask.

"Well, haven't you ever read that witches can't cry?"

"No," Jessica said. "But I didn't know you knew— that I was crying."

"I thought you were. Anyway that proves you're not a witch. At least not now. Maybe you were one and the exorcism sort of backfired. Maybe you exorcised yourself, too."

After Brandon left, Jessica had gone to sleep immediately, with no time to think or decide about anything. She had slept deeply, beyond dreams, and then floated up slowly into consciousness in the dark silence that comes just before dawn.

She lay quietly in the darkness and thought it all through as peacefully as if it had all happened to someone else—without trying to change or forget any part of it. It was a strange way to feel. There was a difference, and she wondered about it. Was it real, would it last?

The crying had been different, too. She wondered if Brandon had really read about witches and crying, or if he had only made it up for the occasion. He was good at things like that.

Dawn was beginning to arrive, and the sky outside the window was a pale pure gray—scrubbed and clean, but still too weary to be blue. Jessica rolled to the side of the bed and looked down at Worm. He was still asleep, but curled now, more normally, in a sleek gray coil.

"Worm," she said, and then she remembered a difference that seemed the most important of all. She remembered the strong real pain she had felt when Brandon said that Worm was dead.

"Worm," she said again, and he sat up quickly, watching her with his long moss-gold eyes. She put her hand out slowly and cautiously and touched his head, and although his ears flickered, he sat still.

"Worm," she said. "I was really sorry you were dead."